FAST BREAK

ALSO BY DEREK JETER

FAST BREAK

DEREK JETER

with Paul Mantell

JETER CHILDREN'S

SIMON & SCHUSTER BOOKS FOR YOUNG READERS

New York   London   Toronto   Sydney   New Delhi

SIMON & SCHUSTER BOOKS FOR YOUNG READERS
An imprint of Simon & Schuster Children's Publishing Division
1230 Avenue of the Americas, New York, New York 10020

SIMON & SCHUSTER BOOKS FOR YOUNG READERS
is a trademark of Simon & Schuster, Inc.
For information about special discounts for bulk purchases, please contact Simon & Schuster Special Sales at 1-866-506-1949 or business@simonandschuster.com.
The Simon & Schuster Speakers Bureau can bring authors to your live event. For more information or to book an event, contact the Simon & Schuster Speakers Bureau at 1-866-248-3049 or visit our website at www.simonspeakers.com.
Book design by Krista Vossen
The text for this book was set in Centennial LT Std.
Manufactured in the United States of America
0319 FFG
First Edition
2 4 6 8 10 9 7 5 3 1
Library of Congress Cataloging-in-Publication Data
Names: Jeter, Derek, 1974– author. | Mantell, Paul, author.
Title: Fast break / Derek Jeter with Paul Mantell.
Description: First edition. | New York : Simon & Schuster Books for Young Readers, [2019] | "Jeter Children's." | Summary: "Young Derek bites off more than he can chew when he decides to enter the school talent show and try out for the basketball team"—Provided by publisher.
Identifiers: LCCN 2018039710| ISBN 9781534436275 (hardback) | ISBN 9781534436299 (eBook)
Subjects: LCSH: Jeter, Derek, 1974——Childhood and youth—Juvenile fiction. | CYAC: Jeter, Derek, 1974——Childhood and youth—Fiction. | Time management—Fiction. | Friendship—Fiction. | Talent shows—Fiction. | Basketball—Fiction. | Baseball—Fiction. | BISAC: JUVENILE FICTION / Sports & Recreation / Baseball & Softball. | JUVENILE FICTION / Sports & Recreation / Basketball. | JUVENILE FICTION / Social Issues / Values & Virtues.
Classification: LCC PZ7.J55319 Fas 2019 | DDC [Fic]—dc23
LC record available at https://lccn.loc.gov/201839710

To those who dare to dream. Don't let fear keep you from working your hardest to reach your goals.

—D. J.

A Note About the Text

The rules of Little League followed in this book are the rules of the present day. There are six innings in each game. Every player on a Little League baseball team must play at least two innings of every game in the field and have at least one at bat. In any given contest, there is a limit on the number of pitches a pitcher can throw, in accordance with age. Pitchers who are eight years old are allowed a maximum of fifty pitches in a game, pitchers who are nine or ten years old are allowed seventy-five pitches per game, and pitchers who are eleven or twelve years old are allowed eighty-five pitches.

Dear Reader,

Fast Break is inspired by some of my experiences growing up. The book portrays the values my parents instilled in me and the lessons they have taught me about how to remain true to myself and embrace the unique differences in everyone around me.

Fast Break is based on the lesson that trying new things is an important part of life and of success; don't be afraid to try, even if you fail. This is one of the principles I have lived by in order to achieve my dreams. I hope you enjoy reading!

Derek Jeter

DEREK JETER'S 10 LIFE LESSONS

1. Set Your Goals High (*The Contract*)

2. Think Before You Act (*Hit & Miss*)

3. Deal with Growing Pains (*Change Up*)

4. The World Isn't Always Fair (*Fair Ball*)

5. Find the Right Role Models (*Curveball*)

6. **Don't Be Afraid to Fail** (*Fast Break*)

7. Have a Strong Supporting Cast

8. Be Serious but Have Fun

9. Be a Leader, Follow the Leader

10. Life Is a Daily Challenge

CONTRACT FOR DEREK JETER

1. Family Comes First. Attend our nightly dinner.
2. Be a Role Model for Sharlee. (She looks to you to model good behavior.)
3. Do Your Schoolwork and Maintain Good Grades (As or Bs).
4. Bedtime. Lights out at nine p.m. on school nights.
5. Do Your Chores. Take out the garbage, clean your room on weekends, and help with the dishes.
6. Respect Others. Be a good friend, classmate, and teammate. Listen to your teachers, coaches, and other adults.
7. Respect Yourself. Take good care of your body and your mind. Avoid alcohol and drugs. Surround yourself with positive friends with strong values.
8. Work Hard. You owe it to yourself and those around you to give your all. Do your best in everything that you do.
9. Think Before You Act.

Failure to comply will result in the loss of playing sports and hanging out with friends. Extra-special rewards include attending a Major League Baseball game, choosing a location for dinner, and selecting another event of your choice.

CONTENTS

Chapter One
TRIPLE CHALLENGE

"It's a rocket to short—OOHH! Jeter makes the diving stab going away from first, then throws from his knees and nails the runner! What a play! That's one for the ages, folks! Let's watch it one more time, in slow motion. . . ."

"Derek! Are you with us?"

Derek Jeter snapped to attention, his beautiful daydream gone in an instant. The whole class full of sixth graders laughed.

"Yes, Ms. Terrapin, I'm listening. Sorry."

"Summer is over, everyone," said the teacher. "I know it's still early September, and it's warm and sunny and beautiful outside—but we've got a lot of work to cover, and I need your attention."

The trouble was, summer *was* over. It felt like a million years since Derek was up at his grandparents' place in Greenwood Lake, New Jersey.

It had been the best summer ever! Derek's best friend Dave Hennum had come for a week to join him. They had played baseball with a bunch of city kids in the Bronx, who would have all been Little League all-stars—if only they'd had a league of their own.

After playing ball with them, Derek's game was better than ever. He couldn't wait to play again! In fact, he'd just gotten caught daydreaming about it.

Too bad his next chance was seven months away. In the meantime, all he could do was play pickup games on Jeter's Hill—the sloping patch of grass in Mount Royal Townhouses, where Derek spent so much of his time that the other kids had named it after him.

In a month or so, cold weather would force everyone else indoors—but not Derek. From October through March, the only kid in Kalamazoo who thought it was warm enough to play baseball was Derek.

He would go to the batting cages with his dad every once in a while, of course, but that was about it. And Derek could feel already that it wouldn't be nearly enough to see him through till spring. No, he was going to have to find something *else* to do until then.

But what?

"Class," said Ms. Terrapin, interrupting his train of

thought, "in a couple of weeks we will be moving forward into the wild worlds of algebra, chemistry, biology, and earth science."

There were murmurings from all around the room. "Ugh. Sounds *hard*," Derek heard Sam Rockman mutter behind him.

"Don't be a wuss," Gary Parnell whispered back to the complainer.

"Lay off him, Gary," Derek said.

Sam shot Derek a silent *Thank you* with his eyes.

Sam Rockman was always scuffling to get a passing grade. He was very nice, but some things took him a little longer to understand—like math. And science.

Gary Parnell, on the other hand, was the class brainiac—which would have been fine, except that he loved to brag about it. Especially to Derek, whom Gary considered his biggest rival.

Gary insisted on making every quiz and every test a contest between the two of them—just to prove who was smarter.

Derek never backed away from the challenge—which was probably why Gary never got tired of beating him. Derek could count on one hand the number of times he'd come out ahead, but that didn't stop him from trying even harder the next time.

On the other hand, when it came to anything involving sports or exercise, Gary usually got a D at best—if not an

F. He always acted like it was torture to break a sweat. Last spring, when he'd been forced to play baseball by his mom and wound up on Derek's team, he'd spent the first three weeks of the season complaining nonstop.

Ms. Terrapin cleared her throat, a signal for the class to quiet down. "Before we move on to sixth-grade work, though, we're going to test what you've already learned. Or at least how much of it you've retained over the summer."

She started passing out test booklets. The kids in front handed them back until they reached the rear of the classroom. Derek noticed that Sam took his reluctantly, with a little shudder of dread.

"As you may know, national standardized tests are coming next spring. They're very different from what you've experienced—and they test everything you've ever learned. So naturally they take a lot of time to prepare for." Another murmur went through the class; a soft ripple of worry.

"So we are giving you a 'pretest.' In addition to giving you valuable practice, it will help us measure your current levels of learning. Don't worry—your scores won't count this time around. But for those of you who are behind and need more help, we'll be recommending after-school study and tutoring between now and next spring."

"Yikes!" said Sam, fidgeting nervously in his seat. "*Extra* study? Tutoring?"

Gary pretended to yawn. "It's good to be a genius," he whispered to Derek. "I get to spend all *my* extra time playing computer games."

"The practice exams will be on September twentieth and twenty-first," said Ms. Terrapin. "One day for English and one day for math. We will be using last year's tests to practice on. Between now and then we will be reviewing for it. I will expect you to go through these study booklets at home."

She stood behind her desk, a gleam in her eye. "Now. Principal Parker has offered a *special pizza party* to the class that does the best. As the world's biggest pizza fan, I expect my class to bring home the pie!"

That got a big cheer—although there were plenty of nervous looks going around too.

"Je-Ter . . . pre-pare to be de-feat-ed!" Gary said, using his best sci-fi robot voice.

"Who's that supposed to sound like?" Derek shot back. "Frankenstein?"

"Don't you know anything? It's *Jar-El*, the final boss!"

"Huh?"

"From *DoomMaster*," Gary explained, as if Derek were a two-year-old and didn't know his fingers from his toes.

"Oooh. Okay," Derek said doubtfully. "Gotta say, I've never heard of *Jar-El*—or *DoomMaster*. Just so you know, though—I am *not* going to be de-feat-ed on this test. Not by Jar-El, and definitely not by you, *Par-Nell*."

Smack-talking was one thing, but actually beating

Gary out on a test that measured *everything they'd ever learned*? That was going to take a lot of extra studying between now and the twentieth!

"Here's something else to take home," said Ms. Terrapin, handing back another bunch of papers. "Applications for the Fall Talent Show."

"Yesss!" Vijay Patel said, pumping his fist. He looked across the room to Derek, waving the form at him excitedly and pointing at it with his other hand.

Derek had completely forgotten about the Fall Talent Show. Now he remembered that he and Vijay had talked about it over the summer—or *written* about it, to be more accurate.

Vijay had been halfway around the world in India last summer, attending a family wedding with his mom and dad—which was why he hadn't joined Derek and Dave at the lake.

Vijay had written though—all about his gigantic family and Indian wedding customs. He'd also suggested the two of them work up a break dance routine for the Fall Talent Show.

Derek had sort of said "okay" . . . then proceeded to forget all about it. But obviously Vijay had *not* forgotten. Not at all.

"All right, class, you can start packing up your things," said the teacher. "The bell's about to—and there it goes," she finished as the bell chimed in right on cue.

"Better start cramming, Jeter," Gary said. "Oh no! Is

that *sweat* on your forehead? You wouldn't be *worried*, now, would you?"

"Not a chance," Derek shot back, showing more confidence than he felt. "Forget *Jar-El*—I am *Je-Ter,* and *you* are going to find out who's the *real* final boss."

"Wait up, Derek!"

Vijay came up to him as he was repacking his book bag in the hallway.

"Hi, Vij."

"So cool, right? You and me in the talent show?" He put out his hand for a high five.

"Definitely," Derek said.

Truth was, the idea of the two of them break-dancing onstage *did* seem like fun. It definitely would make everyone at school stand up and take notice. He and Vijay sometimes fooled around with dance moves when they were over at each other's houses—but nobody at school knew either of them were into it.

If Derek wasn't all that enthusiastic right at the moment, it was because his mind was focused on outscoring Gary on the big test. Creating a talent show act definitely was going to infringe on his study and review time.

"So, let's get going!" Vijay said happily. His parents both worked late at the hospital on Thursdays and wouldn't be home till six, so the two boys had planned to spend the afternoon together at Derek's.

"Last one on the bus is a rotten egg!" Derek said—and the race was on.

Derek got to the school's front lobby way ahead of Vijay. And there was Dave, staring at something posted on the big bulletin board.

"Derek! Check this out!"

Derek looked over his shoulder for Vijay but couldn't see him through the crowd of kids cramming the lobby, all of them trying to get out the door at once.

"What is it?"

"AAU basketball tryouts at the Y!"

"Whoa! Already?"

"A week from Saturday! Are you psyched?"

"Totally!"

"We're gonna have to get our game in gear," Dave said.

Just then a breathless Vijay finally made his way over to them. "I couldn't get through that mob!" he said, laughing. "You are way too fast for me, Derek."

"Hi, Vij," said Dave.

"Hi, Dave. Hey, Derek, we'd better get going. The bus is going to leave without us!"

"Talk to you later, Derek," said Dave, who always got driven home and never took the bus. "We've got to make some plans."

"Definitely!" Derek waved, then followed Vijay out to the bus, his head spinning. Fifteen minutes ago he'd been looking at an easy, relaxed weekend. Now he was looking at a three-ring circus!

Chapter Two

TIME CRUNCH

The two boys sat at Derek's kitchen table, going over their review booklets. Derek's mom was working till six at her accounting job. His dad taught classes at the university in the mornings each weekday as well as three evenings a week, and he had just gotten home.

But at the moment he was still out with Sharlee at her dance class—or was it karate today? Derek couldn't remember—his little sister was even busier than he was. Obviously, though, that was about to change.

"I think we should look over your music collection," Vijay was saying now. "I haven't got nearly as much music as you do."

"Come on, man, we've got to keep studying," Derek said.

"There's a ton of stuff here to review before the twentieth."

"Yes, but we are going to do fine, Derek! We are the best test-takers in the whole class, except for—"

"—for Gary Parnell," Derek finished the sentence. "I know, I know. That's just it."

"I don't get it," said Vijay with a puzzled look.

Derek started to speak, then stopped himself. "Never mind. It's too dumb to even waste time talking about. But I do think we need to keep going over this stuff. I want to make sure we know everything in this booklet backward and forward."

"Okay," said Vijay, backing off. "But maybe we can at least check out some music after? I mean, we *can't* just go up onstage and expect to do a break dance number! We have to plan it all out first and then put in *lots* of time practicing. You know what they say? They say, 'Practice makes perfect!'"

"Well, we'll still have a week after the test . . ."

"Derek, you know all those other kids will be doing stuff they've done for years. We are probably the only ones making up our act from scratch!"

"I know. But—"

"Look, don't worry," Vijay said. "We are both super-good dancers. We just have to figure out what we're going to *do*—and then, of course, practice doing it over and over and over again. If we do that, we are sure to win the contest!"

"Mmm," said Derek. "No pressure, right?"

Vijay laughed. "You are very funny. So what do you say about this weekend? We can figure out our routine, pick out our music . . ."

"Uh . . . sure," Derek said, eager to change the subject. "But right now we need to get back to work."

Being in the talent show was all well and good, but not if it meant having to listen to Gary's mocking *Jar-El* voice for the rest of the semester!

"We were on page twenty-three, at the top. One fourth of one fourth equals . . ."

The phone rang. Derek got up from the kitchen table to answer it.

"Hello?"

"Hey, it's me!"

"Hey, Dave, what's up?"

"When are you free to get together and practice, man? We can use the court at my house this weekend. What do you say?"

Dave lived in a big house with a pool, a golf hole—and, best of all, a tricked-out sports court. And his family had their own personal driver, named Chase, who also served as Dave's guardian whenever his parents were away on business—which was a lot.

"Sure thing! I'll talk to my parents." Derek looked over at Vijay, who was waiting expectantly for him to get off the phone—and he suddenly realized he had a problem. "Uh, listen, Dave, I'm kind of busy right now. Can we talk about it tomorrow?"

He didn't mention to Dave that Vijay was in the room with him. Nor did he say anything that would clue Vijay in to what he and Dave were talking about.

Vijay and Dave were his two best friends—but sometimes it was hard not to make one of them feel like Derek was favoring the other.

"Oh, okay," said Dave. "Talk to you later, then!"

"What was that all about?" Vijay asked after Derek hung up. "He sounded pretty excited."

Derek gave a casual shrug. "Basketball tryouts over at the Y."

"Oh. Yeah, that *is* pretty cool." Vijay smiled, but they both knew that basketball wasn't his sport.

"You . . . you want to try out with us?"

"No, not me. I like baseball and soccer. But basketball? I never understand the dribbling, with only so many steps in between bounces. And the net is too tiny and too far away for my liking!"

Derek laughed. Vijay was always cracking him up.

"Anyway, that's next Saturday, not this one," Vijay went on. "Lucky for us. We'd better put in some time on our act this weekend, don't you think?"

"Yeah. . . ."

Until the moment Ms. Terrapin had handed out their test booklets, Derek's plan for the weekend had been to watch the big Yankees-Tigers series on TV on Saturday, then spend Sunday with his family as usual.

But now, suddenly, everything had been thrown into chaos. He had agreed to meet with two different friends, to practice two different things. And on top of it all, he had to review *everything he'd ever learned* in school—all on Saturday!

It was Mission: Impossible*!*

"So?" Vijay asked.

"Well, it can't be on Sunday . . . that's always family day around here."

"Saturday, then!" Vijay said, smiling. "That's fine. When do you think—morning or afternoon?"

"Um, I'll let you know tomorrow."

"Cool. Let's do our talent show applications before I go."

Just as they finished filling out their forms, the front door opened, and Mr. Jeter came in, followed by Sharlee.

"Hey, you two!" Mr. Jeter greeted them. "What are you up to?"

"Reviewing for a big test," Vijay replied. "And planning our act for the Fall Talent Show!"

"*Talent?*" Mr. Jeter repeated with a twinkle in his eyes. "And which of your many, many talents would that be?"

Derek and Vijay laughed. "Don't tell him—not yet," Derek told Vijay. "It'll be a surprise for you, Dad."

"Tell *me*! Tell *me*!" Sharlee begged, jumping up and down, making her frilly dance skirt bounce along with her.

"No way—you'll just blab to everyone," Derek said, laughing.

"*I will not!* My lips are sealed! See?" She pretended to lock her lips with an invisible key. "Mmm . . . mmmm . . . mmm!"

"Okay, okay, I'll tell you—*later*," Derek conceded. *"Maybe."*

"I'd better get home," Vijay said, gathering up his school stuff. "My parents will be wondering what's keeping me. See you tomorrow, Derek! Don't forget to bring the application with you tomorrow. Bye, all!"

Derek, Sharlee, and Mr. Jeter got to work getting dinner ready. By the time Mrs. Jeter came home, the table was set, the salad made, the vegetables all cut up, and the chicken warming in the oven. All she had to do was drop her briefcase, sit down, and eat!

After dinner Derek helped her dry the dishes. Only when they were done, and the whole family had settled down in the living room, did he bring up his thorny scheduling problem.

"Dad? Mom? Could I go over to Dave's on Saturday afternoon? We need to practice for the under-twelve basketball tryouts."

"Didn't you say you have a lot of reviewing to do?" his mom asked.

"Yes, but it's stuff we've *already learned*. And the test isn't until the twentieth."

"Sometimes we forget a lot over the summer," Derek's dad pointed out. "You told us there's a ton of material to go over. So you need make sure you put aside enough time for it."

"I'm *going* to—a *lot*! But basketball tryouts are next Saturday! Dave and I both want to be on the team, so we need to practice every minute we can between now and then. I can study after that!"

"You're talking about the league down at the Y?" his mom asked.

"Uh-huh. Only the best players make it, Mom! I know Dave and I can do it, though—*if we're prepared enough*. He's got this great sports court at his house. . . ."

Mr. and Mrs. Jeter exchanged glances. "Wouldn't it save you time if Dave came here?" his mom asked.

"Mom, the courts here are all messed up! The rims are bent, and the pavement's cracked. Dave's court is *really awesome*!"

"Wait, now," said his dad. "Didn't you and Vijay say you were preparing something for the talent show? Didn't I hear you tell him you were going to get together on Saturday?"

"There's also the Yankees-Tigers game," Derek added.

"It sounds like you've gotten yourself overcommitted, at least for this weekend," said Mrs. Jeter.

"You said you'd tell me what you were going to do in the show!" Sharlee reminded Derek. "Tell me now! Tell me!"

"We're not even exactly sure yet," Derek confessed to her. "That's why we need to get together," he told his parents. "To figure out what we're going to do."

"It's an awful lot, son," said his dad. "Are you totally sure you want to commit yourself to so many projects? It's hard to do a lot of things well when you're doing them all at once."

"I *am* committed!" Derek insisted. "I mean . . . I'm *pretty sure* I am. . . ."

"So when do you plan to fit all this in?" asked his mom.

"Um . . . that's where I was hoping you could give me some advice," he said.

"Derek," said his dad, "I think you're going to have to eliminate something—at least for this weekend. And it's not going to be our Sunday afternoon, either. We've got a picnic planned, over at the university."

Derek realized there was only one thing he could sacrifice and still keep his commitments. "I guess I won't get to watch the game," he said softly, looking down at the carpet.

Chapter Three

THE SEEDS OF DOUBT

"Yo, Derek!"

Derek turned to see Sam approaching him as he stood at his locker, taking books out of his backpack before heading to class.

"Oh, hey, Sam. What's up?"

"I just wanted to thank you for yesterday," said Sam. "It was . . . well, thank you."

"Aw, that was nothing," Derek said, waving a hand. "Gary acts like such a jerk sometimes. Just ignore him."

"Yeah, that's easy for *you* to say. You always get As and Bs. But me, well . . ." His voice trailed off, and Sam looked down at his shoes.

"Come on, Sam, don't let it get you down. Gary's the one with the problem here."

"It's *not* him, really—it's *me*," said Sam. " Gary's right. I'm just dumb."

"That's a bunch of crud," Derek told him. "You're not dumb—you pass almost every test in class!"

"*Barely.* And I'm going to totally flunk this big practice test, you watch."

"No way, man—we learned all that stuff last year—you knew it back then, right?"

"I totally forgot everything the minute summer came," said Sam. "I've been trying to go over that stupid booklet. But it just makes my eyes cross!"

"Well, don't give up." Derek didn't know what else to say.

"Actually, I was thinking of getting sick on the twentieth," Sam confessed. "Stomach virus or something. It wouldn't be a lie—I'm already half-sick just thinking about it."

"But Ms. Terrapin said the marks don't count on our grades," Derek pointed out.

"*Extra tutoring? Extra study time?* She said that, too, Derek."

"Just give it your best shot. You can't be afraid to fail."

"Speaking of my best shot—I was thinking . . . would you maybe be willing to study with me, like, after school one day?" Sam lived just two buildings over from the Jeters' in Mount Royal Townhouses. "I could walk over to your house, or you could come to mine."

He looked at Derek pleadingly. "Please? I *need* to pass

this test—my mom and dad said if I need extra tutor-ing or after-school study time, I can't play under-twelve basketball!"

"You're trying out?"

"Uh-huh."

"Me too! What position?"

"Point guard. You?"

"Uh . . . point guard."

"Oh. Well . . . good luck. I'm sure you'll get on the team."

"You too," Derek replied.

Sam was definitely the best under-12 player Derek knew. They'd gone one-on-one lots of times, and Sam was more than a little better. His shot was more consistent, he was an outstanding ball handler, and he was a total pain on defense. Derek knew he would be tough compe-tition for the point guard position. And now he was ask-ing Derek's help in passing the test so that he would be allowed to play on the team!

"So . . . what do you say?"

Derek bit his lip. He felt for Sam. Part of him wanted to help. On the other hand, his own schedule was already crammed chock-full.

Of course he had to review the test material anyway. Derek had been thinking of studying with Vijay, who was one of the best students in the class. Studying with Sam would definitely slow down Derek's pace—and eat up more of his scarce time.

"Well, I'm kind of booked this weekend . . ."

"Next week, then? After school?"

"I guess." In the end, he found he couldn't say no. "Well, we'd better get to class," he said with a sigh.

"Right," said Sam. And off they went.

"You've got to be kidding me, Jeter!"

Gary Parnell was staring at the application form in Derek's hand. "*You?* In a *talent show*? I think that's called an 'oxymoron.'"

"Why? You don't think I've got what it takes?" Derek shot back.

"Tsh!" Gary shook his head. "Okay, let's hear it. Are you going to hit a baseball into the audience?"

"I might, if you don't quit yapping."

"Seriously, though—what other talents do you fantasize that you have?"

"Oh, I'm not going to spill the beans—not to you, anyway. I'll just say this—Vijay and I are going to get huge cheers."

"*Vijay?* Oh, please—this is just *too good*!"

"What about *you*, Gary? You too chicken to apply for the show? Or do you only sing in the shower?"

"I would not be caught *dead* on that stage, competing with the rest of you suckers. No way! I am so totally beyond that."

"Yeah. Beyond the beyond."

"But I'll tell you one thing, Jeter," Gary said as Derek got up from his desk to hand in the application. "I'm going to park myself right there in the front row. I want to get a good close-up view of you when everyone is laughing at you!"

Derek ignored him—or at least he didn't answer Gary or even turn around to dignify that last rude comment. He knew Gary was that way about everything—except for the things *he* liked, like math, chess, and now computer games.

Still, what if Gary was right about Derek and Vijay's dance? What if they did bomb up there onstage?

Gary, in his sneaky way, had somehow succeeded in planting a tiny seed of doubt in Derek's brain.

Suddenly, agreeing to be in the talent show seemed like a bad idea. Still, he'd promised Vijay he'd do it. Second thoughts or not, Derek was going to get up there on that stage and give it everything he had.

"Class," said Ms. Terrapin when they'd all settled back in their seats, "Since I know you're all working hard reviewing the material in your booklets, I'm going to go light on homework this weekend—"

"*Homework*?!" Sam moaned. "She's giving us *homework, too*?"

"Yes!" said the teacher as if she had supersonic hearing. "Just because we're reviewing, that doesn't mean we can stop moving forward. But don't worry—this weekend, it's only an essay. I want two full double-spaced pages from each of you—on the subject of 'My Animal Encounter.'"

A groan went up from several of the students—Derek included. "We don't have to get up and read them out loud in front of the class, do we?" he asked.

If there was one thing Derek was most scared of, it was getting up and speaking in front of a roomful of people.

"Not this time," said Ms. Terrapin, and Derek breathed a sigh of relief. "But we *will* be doing a public speaking unit later this semester."

Derek winced. Looking over at Sam, he saw that the poor guy had his head in his hands.

Derek knew there was no way he could back out of helping Sam, any more than he could back out of the talent show after promising Vijay.

Derek hadn't had a chance to talk to him all morning. But the two friends caught up later that morning, at recess.

"So how is tomorrow afternoon for you?" Vijay asked eagerly.

"Uh, not good. Sorry—I'm already booked."

"Booked?"

Derek had been dreading this moment, but there was no way of avoiding it any longer. "Yeah . . . um, my mom is driving me over to Dave's . . . to practice basketball."

Vijay's shoulders slumped. "Derek, I know you want to

make the team—but you *will*! You're so good at basketball already! And we haven't even picked out our music, let alone put together a routine, and practiced it at least a dozen times."

"Yeah, but tryouts are next Saturday, Vij—and the show's not till October eighth. We'll have plenty of time before then."

"I'm glad you think so," said Vijay, clearly disappointed. "I'm not as confident as you are."

Derek wasn't that confident onstage himself—but he didn't try to argue. He had known Vijay would be upset. He would have been too, if their roles had been reversed.

"So when *can* you get together this weekend?"

"Um, how's Saturday night?" Derek asked.

"No good for me. It's a big celebration at our Hindu temple," Vijay explained.

"At least you'll be having some fun," Derek said. "How's Sunday night, then? Okay?"

"I guess so," Vijay said, clearly down in the dumps. "But we'd better make a lot of headway."

"Your house or mine?"

"Yours," said Vijay. "I'll bring a few songs, but you've got a much bigger selection."

"Deal," said Derek. "And don't worry—we're going to be great!"

Vijay smiled and headed back inside to the cafeteria. Derek lingered awhile, watching some older kids shooting hoops at the other end of the playground.

Derek had told his friend they were going to be great, and it had made Vijay a little happier. But inside he kept hearing Gary's mocking words: "I want to get a good close-up view of you when everyone is laughing at you!"

The tiny seed of doubt Gary had planted in Derek's brain was growing like a noxious weed.

Chapter Four

HOOP DREAMS

"And he drops another 3! Jeter is on fire!"

Dave was playing announcer for Derek, and vice versa, as they practiced their shooting on Dave's spectacular court.

Behind them was the small golf hole his mom and dad had put in, so that whenever he wanted to, Dave could practice the game that was his life's true passion.

Of course Derek's sport was *baseball*, not basketball. But that didn't mean he didn't love basketball, too. "From now on I'm going to bring a ball with me wherever I go and dribble my way down the street," he told Dave. "Got to make it second nature, you know?"

"I hear you," Dave said. "Here, let me have that."

Derek handed him the ball, and Dave started taking a

few shots. Most of them caromed off the rim or the back-board, and a few just caught air. "You need more arc on your shot," Derek told him.

"More arc?"

"Yeah, you know—think of a rainbow."

"Like this?"

He took another shot, and this time, swished it.

"There you go," said Derek, giving his friend a fist bump. "Here, give me that ball."

They kept on taking turns—shooting from all distances and angles, taking free throws and layups, playing pick-and-roll with invisible opponents, and going one-on-one.

"Okay, break time," Dave said breathlessly at last. It was a hot, sunny September day, and they'd been at it for over an hour. Both boys were pouring sweat and breath-ing hard. "Let's get in the shade and have a cold drink."

There was a covered bench at the side of the court, and Derek and Dave sat down and took water bottles out of a cooler.

"Aaahhh," said Dave. "Wow. That was a workout!"

"Tell me about it!"

"We've got to do this every day between now and next Saturday."

"I wish I could," Derek said. "But I've got too much going on most of the time."

"Hey, I've got schoolwork too, man. But if we want to make this team, we need to be at the top of our game!"

"It's not just schoolwork—Vijay and I have to work up our thing for the talent show."

"Derek—remember last summer when we talked about playing for Saint Augustine's in seventh grade? Being part of that great basketball tradition—having our pictures up on that wall in the hallway, with all the trophies in the glass cases?"

"Yeah."

"You know who coaches the under-twelve team?"

"No—who?"

"Mr. Nelson!"

Mr. Nelson, who was, of course, *also* the coach of the Saint Augustine basketball team. "If we make this team, we're a cinch to play for the Irish next year!"

Derek sat silently, pondering how he could carve out some more time to come out here. Dave's family lived way out on the outskirts of town.

"Of course, if the talent show's that important to you . . ."

"It's not that. . . ." Derek was going to explain how much Vijay was looking forward to doing the talent show with him. But he decided to keep that part to himself. He didn't want to drag Vijay into it or set up conflict between his two best friends in the world.

"I just thought it would be fun to give it a shot, you know?" he said. "I just didn't think it was going to get in the way of basketball tryouts."

"You could back out of it," Dave said. "It's not too late."

"No, I don't think so. I'm going to have to find some way to make it all happen."

"How?"

Derek sighed. "That's the part I haven't figured out yet."

He finished his water, put down the bottle, and stood up. "Come on," he said. "Let's get back to work. I'm going to drive on you, and you have to block my shot, or make me miss, and come down with the rebound."

Dave was tall and thin and athletic. He had a good vertical leap and long arms—good for blocking shots and rebounding. But he wasn't bulky enough to go toe-to-toe with other teams' big men. Derek thought he would make a good small forward—but that meant improving his jump shot first.

Derek tried showing him, demonstrating proper form, but Dave didn't seem to get it. And when he tried and failed, he was quick to go right back to the old, wrong way of doing it.

Derek could see that Dave needed more coaching than he could give him. And that gave him a great idea. . . .

"*I've got it!*" he suddenly shouted, leaving Dave unguarded in the middle of driving to the basket.

Dave buried the easy layup and said, "Hey! What happened?"

"I know how we can improve our game in a hurry."

"Cool! How?"

"Are you busy tomorrow afternoon?"

"Um, I don't think so . . . why?"

"I'm going for a picnic with my folks and Sharlee at the college where my dad works. They've got indoor and outdoor courts there, and we sometimes fool around on them if nobody else is playing."

"I get it—if I'm there—"

"Right! You and I can get our practice in, and my dad will be right there to coach us! Except . . . you're not invited—*yet*."

"Oh man, I hope they say yes!"

"I'll ask them as soon as I get home. Speaking of which, what time is it now?"

Dave checked his watch. "Ten to five."

"Yikes! My dad's picking me up in ten minutes."

"Have we got enough time for more game? We can play to 11 instead of 21."

Derek grinned. "Let's go for it!"

"Dad? Mom? Could I ask you guys a huge, huge favor?"

That got his parents' attention. They'd been sitting in the living room together after supper, with Derek's dad going over his lesson plans, Mrs. Jeter playing checkers with Sharlee—and Derek trying to think of how to ask what he was about to ask.

"How huge is huge?" his mom quipped.

"Well, not *that* huge, really—but it is kind of last minute. I was hoping you guys would be okay if Dave joined us tomorrow afternoon?"

"I don't understand, Derek," his dad said. "Why is it so important?"

"Well, we need to keep on practicing hoops every day this week, because tryouts are next weekend . . ."

". . . and the college has the best courts around," his dad finished for him.

"But that's not all of it," Derek went on. "Dave and I need you to coach us. You know, get us ready for next Saturday."

"Hmmm," said his dad. "Weren't you also supposed to be doing something with Vijay?"

"He's coming over *after dinner* tomorrow—we've got to go through our music for the talent show."

"Music? There's music in it?" Sharlee said, eyes wide. "Tell me! I can't stand it anymore!"

"I told you, nosey, we haven't even decided yet," Derek said. "When we do, you'll be the first one to know, okay?"

"Yay!" said Sharlee, satisfied for now.

"And you've got your big tests coming up too, right?" his mom asked.

"Yes, but I've already got study time blocked out," Derek assured her.

Actually, he hadn't exactly marked down times on a calendar or anything like that—but he was committed to putting in time studying for the tests—he hadn't forgotten for a minute about Gary Parnell's challenge.

"Besides," he added, "if Dave and I can practice

tomorrow, it'll leave more time for studying later on!" He wasn't sure how, or when—but there had to be an hour in there somewhere.

"Derek, if you're going to spend time with Dave tomorrow, I don't want it to be at the expense of our family time. I'm fine with him coming along—but anything we do tomorrow is going to include *all* of us." Mrs. Jeter inclined her head in Sharlee's direction.

"If Derek's friend is coming, I want Ciara to come too!" Sharlee protested.

"It's too late to arrange that, Sharlee," Mrs. Jeter said. "But we can take Ciara along another time, okay?"

"Awww . . ." Sharlee pouted and folded her arms across her chest.

"If I'm going to coach you and Dave," said Derek's dad, "then Sharlee's going to be my assistant coach. Right, Sharlee?"

"Yay!" Sharlee said, suddenly forgetting to be sad. "I get to tell Derek what to do!"

They all laughed, and Derek said, "Thanks, you guys— that's awesome! I've got to go call Dave and let him know!"

"Tell him to get here at eleven thirty," his mom called after him. "We're heading over to the college around noon."

After lining everything up with Dave, Derek said good night to everyone and went upstairs to work on his essay before bedtime.

"'My Animal Encounter'?" he said to himself as he stared at the empty page in front of him. "I've never had any pets. We don't live in the woods. What am I supposed to write about?"

He sighed deeply, but he knew it was no use to moan and groan. Complaining to his empty room wasn't going to get him out of it. He looked at his alarm clock—the red numbers said 9:30. Derek blew out another breath. He was going to have to find something embarrassing to share, and fast.

AARRGH! *His mind was a total blank!*

He knew there must be dozens of times he'd crossed paths with animals—at the zoo, around the neighborhood— so why couldn't he think of any now, when he needed to?

His mind was running through memories, one after the other. They started to blend together . . . and at some point, they turned into a dream. . . .

Derek shook himself awake and stared at the alarm clock—it was past ten!

His brain was totally fried. There was no way he could possibly write this stupid essay when he was this tired!

Still, he knew he had to try. He'd already committed tomorrow morning to reviewing for the test.

Make something up! he told himself. But even that proved difficult.

Finally, around ten thirty, he remembered the time he

and a couple of his friends found that stray cat near the Mount Royal Townhouses' maintenance shed. They named her Miss Jiggy, built a little house for her out of pieces of wood and asphalt shingles, and brought her food and water every day. This went on for almost a week. And then one day Miss Jiggy simply disappeared. The boys went crazy trying to find her, but they never did—until months later, when Derek saw Miss Jiggy looking at him from the neighbor's kitchen window—wearing a satisfied cat smile and a jeweled collar around her neck!

It wasn't much of an animal adventure, Derek thought—but it would have to do. He got to work, scribbling as fast as he could, struggling to keep his eyes open. . . .

"Derek?"

Derek woke up suddenly and realized he'd fallen asleep at his desk. His light was still on from the night before, and his alarm clock showed 9:45—*a.m.!*

"I'm awake," he said sleepily.

"Breakfast is ready. It's late—weren't you going to do some review this morning?"

"Uh . . . yeah. Be right down."

Derek felt a sense of panic rise from his stomach up through his chest. *His essay!*

Staring at the paper, he saw that he hadn't even filled up half a page before falling asleep last night.

He had to finish it before Dave got there!

He washed up, got dressed, ran downstairs, ate breakfast, ran back up to his room, and scribbled away madly for half an hour until he'd finished his essay. Then he looked up at the clock—five to eleven! Dave would be there in half an hour!

Derek looked down at what he'd written. The essay was long enough, at least. But his handwriting was totally messed up—it looked like a crazy person had written it—and when he read it over, he realized that he'd mixed up the order of events. His teacher would definitely lower his mark if he didn't rewrite the whole thing—*neatly*.

Derek set to work, knowing he'd blown it royally. This was going to take up the rest of his reviewing time. Unless he called things off with Vijay for tonight—and he'd already done that once this weekend—there would be no time for studying this weekend.

Derek gave in to the grim reality. He would just have to put in double duty studying during the week.

Of course, that would cut into his *other* commitments—the ones he cared about the most. But there was no time to think about that now.

Derek let out a big yawn, shook his head to get the cobwebs out, and started rewriting his essay.

Chapter Five

FEAR FACTOR

"Thanks, Dr. and Mrs. Jeter—that was delicious," Dave said, getting up from the picnic table. He and Derek had already finished their sandwiches and drinks, and they were anxious to start practicing as soon as they could.

But the rest of Derek's family were barely halfway through their lunches, so the two boys busied themselves cleaning up the leftovers and paper goods.

"Glad you liked it, Dave. You can thank Sharlee, too— she helped spread the peanut butter and jelly."

"Hey, good job, Sharlee!" Dave said with a grin. Sharlee smiled back, though her mouth was too full of PB and J and bread to answer.

The courts at Western Michigan University were just a

short distance from the picnic area. Derek spotted a court that wasn't occupied. Dribbling his basketball all the way, he raced over to claim it before anyone else got there.

"Okay, let's get a look at your game," said Derek's dad. "Start by taking some layups."

"I'll feed you the ball," said Mrs. Jeter.

"What do *I* get to do?" Sharlee asked.

"You get all the rebounds, okay?" said Mr. Jeter.

"Yay!"

Sharlee might have been too short to put the ball through the hoop, but she was determined to be in the game. She was certainly athletic—that much was clear. She already had a feel for dribbling and was fast and agile. Not to mention the fact that she could dance *and* break boards with one swift kick!

After a few passes at the basket, Mr. Jeter had the boys run the length of the court side by side, passing the ball back and forth between them until one took the layup.

"Now switch it up," Mr. Jeter told them.

A few more passes, and everyone needed to stop for a drink and a breather. The day was hot—summer hadn't quite let go yet.

"I notice both of you are way more comfortable coming from your right side and dribbling with your right hand. So I want you to concentrate on your left-hand dribble this week. You've got to be able to drive both sides of the basket."

"I can do that already!" Sharlee said proudly, taking the ball from her father and showing them all how she could dribble with both her hands, not just one.

"Very good, Sharlee," said Mrs. Jeter, and they all applauded.

"Daddy, pick me up so I can shoot it!" Mr. Jeter did as he was told, and Sharlee basked in a second round of applause.

"Okay, how about a little three-on-two?" said Mr. Jeter. "Me and Dave versus Dot, Derek, and Sharlee."

Everyone got into the scrimmage. Mr. and Mrs. Jeter guarded each other, allowing Derek and Dave to face off, while Sharlee hung out beneath the basket, ready to scoop up any and all rebounds.

Dave might not have been a good shooter, but he sure could play D. With his long arms outstretched, he made it difficult for Derek to get off a shot—or even make a decent pass. Derek had to work hard to fake him out, so he could get the ball under or over or around those waving arms.

On defense, though, Derek gave as good as he got. He wasn't as tall as Dave—but he was faster, with quicker reactions, and a good feel for what Dave would try next.

For the first ten minutes, the score stayed low—it reached 3–2 in favor of Derek's team, then stayed there as possession went back and forth. Dave would clank a shot off the rim, and Derek would snag the rebound. Or Derek would take a wild, long jumper and catch only air, with his dad grabbing the ball back for the other side.

Then Derek caught fire, finding his shooting touch and running off four straight baskets! "Whoo-hoo!" Sharlee yelled, her arms raised in triumph. "Derek's on fire!"

But just when it looked like the game was decided, Mr. Jeter and Dave kicked their games into high gear. Dave stole the ball from Derek and sank an uncontested layup. Then Mr. Jeter blocked a shot from Mrs. Jeter and found Dave for another easy put-in.

"Time out!" Sharlee shouted. "We need a break!"

"Good idea," Mrs. Jeter said. "Come on, everyone. Drink some water. It's hot out here."

They soon resumed their game, and now it had gotten serious. Everyone was putting their utmost effort into it—including Sharlee, who actually stole the ball from her dad when he wasn't looking her way.

"Great job, Sharlee!" Derek said as he took the pass from her—and right before Dave grabbed it away from him and sank a jumper to bring their team within one point of Derek's side.

The scrimmage remained close most of the way, with the lead switching back and forth. In the end, Derek's team won out, with Derek sinking a couple of difficult shots to ice the victory, 21–18.

Sharlee wound up with the most rebounds and held on to the ball at the end as she went into her victory dance.

"We would have won if I'd shot better," Dave said as

they all sat on a shaded bench at courtside, drinking water. "I just can't seem to get the feel for it."

"You hit that one tough shot," Derek said.

"Yeah, but that was just dumb luck," Dave replied. "I couldn't hit that one again if I tried."

"Let me have a closer look at what you're doing," Mr. Jeter said, getting up and beckoning Dave to follow. "The rest of you relax for a few minutes."

Derek watched as his dad worked with Dave on transferring from the dribble to the shooting position. He showed him how to roll the ball off the fingertips and end with a flick of the hand toward the rim. He told Dave to put more of an arc into his shot. And he made sure he was vertical and balanced when he went up for the jump shot.

By the end of their short session, Dave was at least coming close every time. He was throwing up fewer bricks and fewer air balls, and even swishing a couple of shots along the way.

"You keep practicing that all week, until it's second nature," Mr. Jeter said as they came back to join the others. "It's going to come, but it takes time and repetition."

"What about *me*?" Derek asked. "What should I be concentrating on this week?"

"First of all, like I said, you need to be dribbling with your left hand and driving the lane from the left side, taking layups from the left. Second, you've got some nice deceptive moves, but you've got to make sure that, when you go up for the shot, you're staying in balance—not falling back or forward or tilting to one side. That's why your shot drifts sometimes. So make sure to plant your push-off foot firmly."

Derek knew his father was right. He'd seen many of his shots hit the rim after drifting to the left. He would have to work on that this week—whenever he could find a minute.

"Okay, check this song out—it's 'Fresh.'"

"I'll bet it is," Derek said.

"No, that's the *name* of it—'Fresh.' It's by Kool and the Gang." Vijay hit the play button, and the song began.

"It *is* cool," Derek said, nodding his head to the beat as he imagined moves he could do along with it. He was lying on his bed, propped up by a bunch of pillows. He had zero energy left after his long, hot afternoon playing basketball in the sun.

After listening for a while, he said, "What else have you got?"

"I've already played you six different songs," Vijay said. "I've only got one left." Sighing, he switched to another. "This one's called 'Smalltown Boy.' It's by Bronski Beat—they're British—and it was number one for three weeks in a row."

Derek listened as the beat took hold. "Yeah, I like this groove—but I don't know, Vij—we're not exactly small-town boys. Kalamazoo is not a small town."

"Well, okay, but it's not New York or London or Mumbai either," Vijay pointed out.

"We've got to at least come off slick, y'know? If we're going to do the chicken dance and stuff, I don't want people thinking we're a couple of yokels or something."

"I don't get you, Derek," Vijay said, taking out the CD. "You've got a problem with every song I brought. Are you in a bad mood or something?"

"I'm just tired. I didn't sleep much last night." That much was definitely true. But he didn't mention that he'd also played basketball that afternoon.

"Well, tired or not, we've got to pick a song so we can start planning out our routine! So since you don't like any of my music, what have you got in your collection?"

Derek had told Vijay he would look through his music before tonight—but he just hadn't had the time!

Now he was at a loss for words. He looked over his collection but didn't see anything that really excited him. Some of the songs were too slow for break dancing, some weren't high-powered enough—and some, he'd just plain gotten tired of.

In fact, the whole *idea* of being in the talent show was beginning to feel tiring. And beyond that, there was something else bothering Derek about it.

He'd told Vijay he was tired, but really, it was more than that. While being in the show had sounded like a fun idea way back in the summer, Derek now found himself getting cold feet. That little seed of doubt Gary had planted in his brain had begun to grow and flower.

Derek had never performed on a stage before—ever. What if he messed up royally? What if the audience laughed at him?

Still, he didn't want to let Vijay down. Besides, he didn't want to feel like he was running away.

"Well? What have you got?" Vijay said impatiently, bouncing his knees up and down with pent-up energy. Obviously, he hadn't been losing sleep over anything like Derek had.

Derek knew his friend must have sensed that something was wrong. Vijay always seemed to know what was in Derek's heart. He was going to have to be honest—but maybe not just yet . . . he had to find a way to explain his second thoughts without upsetting Vijay. . . .

"*Derek? Vijay?*" It was Derek's mom, calling up from downstairs. "Time to wrap it up, guys. It's getting late!"

Saved by the bell, thought Derek. *Whew!*

Vijay sighed. "So when can we get back to it?" he asked.

"I'll . . . let you know tomorrow, okay? I've got to see what this week looks like."

"But—"

"We'll do it *soon*, don't worry," he assured Vijay. "And I'll have the song picked by then."

"Don't I get a vote?" Vijay protested.

"Of course! But I *know* you're going to *love* it."

Derek sure *hoped* so. Because he had no idea what song he was going to pick!

After seeing Vijay out, Derek went back upstairs. It was already late, but he still needed to put in some time going over the test review booklet.

He sat down at his desk and tried to concentrate—but it was too hard. He was dog-tired, and his eyes kept wanting to close.

"Derek?"

His mom, a look of concern in her eyes, was standing in the open doorway. "It's past ten. You've got school tomorrow."

"I have to study, Mom," he protested.

"You should have gotten that done earlier," she countered. "You know studying has to come first."

"But we had our family picnic!"

"There were other times this weekend, old man." She came into the room and sat down on the side of his bed. "Your dad and I were talking about it—you're doing so much, you seem all stressed out."

Derek heaved a huge sigh. "Totally," he said with a weary edge to his voice. "But it's all stuff I really want to do!"

"Are you sure?"

"I really, really want to make this team, Mom! Only the best players get into AAU league."

"And the talent show?"

"It'll be fun—if we ever get our act together. Anyway, I promised Vijay. I just wish the two things weren't happening at the same time. And then there's this big test on top of it! Why did Ms. Terrapin have to assign us an essay, too—this weekend of all weekends?"

"It's not her fault if you've got other things on your plate besides school," said his mom. "Derek, if you really want to do it all, you're going to have to manage your time better. And in the end, you may find it really is all too much. In that case, something will have to go by the wayside."

"No! I mean, I don't want to drop anything."

"Well, then, let's check out this upcoming week." She got up and took a look at Derek's wall calendar, which hung over his desk, right next to the poster of Dave Winfield, the Yankees right fielder, who was Derek's idol.

"Let's see . . . basketball tryouts are Saturday . . . testing is when?"

"The twentieth and twenty-first."

"That's Monday and Tuesday. And the talent show?"

"Not till October eighth—but we don't even have any ideas yet. We haven't even picked out music! Vijay is already freaking out about it."

"Well, he's wise to be thinking ahead, at any rate. Still, it seems like there's more give there. You still have three weeks to prepare. Maybe you and Vijay could do some planning over the phone this week and really go at it after testing is done."

"It's not that simple, Mom," Derek said. "This Saturday's basketball tryouts are only the first round. There's a second round the Saturday after, so there goes another week—*if* I get that far."

"Well, you can cross that bridge when you come to it. Meanwhile, I suggest you work things out with Vijay so that you're both okay with the plan. As for basketball, as long as you've left enough time for schoolwork, I'm sure you and Dave can find time to practice."

"But we both need Dad to keep coaching us, and he's only around at certain times."

"Hmmm. Well, you'll have to work that out with him—but remember, we also have to get Sharlee to her dance and karate classes. Let me go get him, so you two can figure things out."

Derek closed his review book and got ready for bed. He had just finished brushing his teeth when his dad came in.

"Mom tells me you want me to work with you and Dave this week."

"Can you, Dad? Please?"

"Well, tomorrow Sharlee has dance class, and Tuesday she's got karate. But that's over at five. Evenings are out—I've got papers to grade, and you've got homework and studying. I could do an hour with you boys on Wednesday and Thursday after school. But there wouldn't be time to get down to the college. It would have to be on the courts here at home."

"Awww . . ."

"Don't worry about what shape the *courts* are in—worry about the shape your *game* is in," his dad advised. "You can't play your best basketball if you've got six other things going through your head at the same time."

"Okay, Dad. Thanks. I'll tell Dave about Wednesday and Thursday."

"Listen, Derek—I know you've got a lot on your mind, but you need to get your rest, too. If you're tired, you won't be able to give it your best, either in school or on the basketball court."

"I can't stop thinking about those tryouts," Derek said.

"Well, then just think this one thing—you might not be the most talented kid trying out. But if you get your rest, you can at least make sure you *outwork* everybody else. And in the end, that's what's going to put you over the top."

Derek hugged his father. "Thanks, Dad," he said.

"Good night, old man. Get some rest. You've been on overdrive all week."

"I will. G'night."

Derek wished he could have dropped everything else, just for this one week, and concentrate totally on basketball. But he knew his dad was right. From now on, he promised himself, he was going to plan his time carefully. Otherwise, he was going to burn out—and that could mean failing at everything he was trying to do!

Chapter Six
PRESSURE COOKER

Derek had dribbled his basketball left-handed all the way from the school bus into the building and down the hallway. Now he was trying to fit it inside his locker without having it roll back out.

"Hey! Derek! What's up?"

"Sam!" he said, turning around. "Not much. What's up with you?"

He had a sinking feeling he knew exactly what was up with Sam.

"So how's this afternoon?" Sam said. "I really need to start *studying*."

Wait, wait, thought Derek. *He hasn't even started?*

Derek was trapped, and he knew it. He'd said he would

help Sam study. Then he'd forgotten all about it!

Well, what could he say now? He was going to be spending that afternoon studying anyway. And Sam lived just two buildings over in Mount Royal Townhouses.

Derek knew his parents wouldn't object. Sam and Derek had known each other for years, and their parents often stopped for a friendly chat in the parking lot. But he also knew that it would take way more time to wade through the work with Sam around.

On the other hand, Sam needed his help, and he'd already offered to give it.

"Um, I guess you could come over for a while."

"Thanks!" Sam said, clapping him on the shoulder. He walked off down the hall, and Derek stared after him, shaking his head.

So now he was going to help Sam do well on the tests. So that Sam's mom would let him play basketball for the under-12 team. At point guard—the very position Derek was aiming for! If Sam made the team at point guard, it would probably mean there was no spot for Derek. And, as Derek well knew, Sam was a real sharpshooter from long range. His own shot was *pretty* good, but not *that* good.

He needed to work on his shot this week! His dad had promised him and Dave two hours, but that wasn't going to be nearly enough!

"Hey, Jeter—what are you staring at?" Gary stood at Derek's shoulder, following his gaze and spotting Sam bouncing happily down the hall. "So. You and 'Rockhead' are new best buds, huh? A little birdie told me you two are going to be *studying* together. It can't be true, can it? Please—say it isn't so, Jeter!"

"You're unbelievable, Parnell," Derek said, shaking his head in wonder. "What do you care who I study with?"

Gary shrugged. "Whoa. Touchy, aren't we? Well, suit yourself, big man. Happy studying."

"I suppose you study alone, huh?"

Gary snorted. "Me? I ripped through that stupid review booklet in twenty minutes, then tossed it in the newspaper recycling. Jar-El and I had a date with destiny."

"Huh. Interesting. Not getting too overconfident, are you, Gar? You might wind up sorry you tossed that booklet, my man."

"Not a chance," Gary said, chuckling. "You two can study up the wazoo from now till test time, but Sam's *still* going to fail. As for you, you'll *probably* pass—but as for beating my score? Dream on, Jeter. I'm going to wipe the floor with you—in math *and* English."

Derek was about to argue some more, but the two-minute bell rang, and they both had to scurry to get to class on time.

"We didn't get to talk this morning," Vijay said as they stood in the cafeteria line at lunch. "What songs did you come up with?"

"Um, I've, uh, got a couple to play for you."

"What are they?"

"They're . . . no, it's better if you just hear them without me blowing the surprise," Derek said.

He was making this all up as he went—not having even a vague idea of which songs he might want to suggest. He just needed a little more time to come up with something!

"So, can we meet after school?" Vijay asked, a slight note of frustration in his voice.

"Um, no, actually—not today. I've got to spend the afternoon reviewing for the test, because I didn't get it done over the weekend."

Vijay sighed. "Man, I'm starting to wonder if you really want to do this with me. . . ."

"I do!" Derek said quickly. "It's just . . ."

He took a deep breath. There was no sense evading things any longer.

"Look, Vij, I'll level with you. I've just got too much on my plate this week. After the test and tryout I'll have more time."

"But that would leave just two weeks!" Vijay said. "We don't want to get up there onstage and do something half-baked. We want to win this thing! The whole enchilada!"

"Speaking of which," Derek said, "look what's for lunch."

"Enchiladas—ha!" The two boys shared a laugh. "Seriously, though, Derek—we need to nail what song we're doing, like, right away. Can't we meet after school for a little while? You can study later tonight, can't you?"

"That's not how it works around my house," Derek said, although Vijay, as an old friend, already knew that in the Jeter household, nothing happened until the homework was done.

"We could study together!" Vijay suggested, but Derek shook his head.

"Not unless you want to study with Sam Rockman, too. He's coming over after school to study with me."

"What? But—"

"It's no use—I promised him I'd help him go over everything."

"Oh. I see," said Vijay, clearly disappointed.

"I couldn't stand the way Gary was making fun of him, so I . . . well, you get the idea."

Vijay nodded. "I get it," he said. "You're doing a good thing, Derek. But aren't you busy enough?"

"You're not telling me anything I don't already know," Derek said as they walked to a table. "But I had to study anyway."

"We two could have gotten through it a lot faster."

"True. But then, where would that leave Sam? I couldn't stand it if Gary got to fire away at him after this big test."

"Yeah, I get it," Vijay said. "Too bad. But okay. So when can we get together?"

"Well, we could do an hour on Tuesday, after Sharlee's karate class . . ."

"One hour?" Vijay frowned. "Okay, I guess, but that's not much time. What about Wednesday?"

"Um, listen, Vij, there's something else I have to tell you about—something else that's competing for my time. You know I'm trying out for the under-twelve basketball team at the Y on Saturday. With Dave. Sooo . . . we've got to practice before that, and my dad's going to give us some pointers. Except he's only free Wednesday and Thursday afternoons between 3:30 and 4:30. Which leaves only about an hour for us those afternoons, too. Sorry."

Vijay shook his head sadly. "I see," he said. "And you did not want to tell me."

"I thought it might hurt your feelings," Derek admitted. "I guess I wound up doing that anyway. Sorry."

Vijay heaved a deep sigh. "I know you love basketball," he said. "And being in a talent show . . . it's the first time. You must be nervous about it."

"No! I'm not nervous—it's not that. It's . . ." Derek's voice petered out.

He definitely did not want to go up there onstage and look bad. And he knew Vijay was right—if they wanted to succeed, they had to put in the work.

"Let's talk tonight over the phone," Derek suggested. "I can play you the songs, and you can decide. And as soon as the tests are over, we can put time into it almost every day, okay?"

Vijay looked up at Derek, and a smile appeared at the

corner of his mouth. "Okay," he said. "Call me after supper. I sure hope you've picked us a winner."

Derek swallowed hard. He hadn't picked anything—nothing at all.

"I . . . don't know. $6,243?"

Derek shook his head sadly. "No, Sam. It's B—$62.43. See, you can't forget the decimal point."

"Right, right . . ." Sam shook his head. "It's just so hard to get. Why is it there again?"

Derek tried not to show his impatience. They'd been going over math for an hour already, and they were still on the same page they'd started on. Derek had been racking his brain, trying to come up with a way to explain it to Sam, but nothing seemed to work.

And this was stuff Derek had already gone through! He hadn't devoted one second today to the stuff he still needed to review, much farther on in the booklet.

"Think of it this way," he said, an idea coming to him. "You're dribbling the ball across midcourt, and the forward is coming out to set a pick for you, okay?"

"Yeah?" Sam said, nodding.

"So where the forward sets the pick matters, right?"

"Of course! If he sets it too far out, like at the three-point line, I can drive around him and look for an outlet if I'm double-teamed. If he sets it too close to the basket, then back off a step and sink the open jumper."

"Exactly!" Derek said. "So that's how it is with decimal points—if the numbers are to the left of them, they're whole numbers. If they're to the right of the decimal point, they're fractions, or percentages."

"Oh. Wow—I never thought of it that way before. So, like, whatever is to the right of it is a percentage of one?"

"Yessss!!" Derek cried triumphantly, doing a fist pump. "Sam, we're definitely making progress. Now, let's get back to the booklet—"

"Uh . . . maybe tomorrow," said Sam. "My brain is totally fried, man. And my stomach's rumbling too. Gotta get some dinner in there fast." He grinned at Derek and reached down for his book bag.

He yanked up on the strap, but he'd forgotten to zip up the bag, and as he lifted it, something fell out—a portable CD player. It popped open, revealing the CD inside.

Derek gasped. "That's it!"

"Huh?" Sam reached down for the CD player.

"Wait, Sam—can I borrow that disc?"

"*Thriller*? I don't know, man, it's my favorite. It never gets old."

Derek nodded. *Thriller*, the album, had been at the top of the charts all of last year. Yet Derek had never thought of it till now. And the title song was *perfect* for him and Vijay!

"Please? I'll study with you again tomorrow."

"Well, in that case . . . okay—but take good care of it. I'll be wanting it back soon."

"Can I have it till the talent show?" Derek begged.

"Whoa. That's three weeks away. Mmmm . . ."

Never mind, thought Derek. He could buy his own copy with the money he'd saved out of his allowance. "Okay, just for a couple days."

"Sure. Here y'go."

"Thanks, Sam. You're a lifesaver!"

"Really? Cool! Well, gotta go—see you after school tomorrow!"

"Yeah . . . tomorrow."

Derek wasn't thrilled about doing all this studying with Sam, but he knew he was doing the right thing. And now his generosity had been rewarded—because of it, he'd found the perfect song for him and Vijay!

"Okay, so what songs did you find?"

"Not songs—*song*. This is going to be the one, Vij. Check it out."

He popped the CD into his player and put the phone up to it so Vijay could hear. He let it play for half a verse, then paused it and put the phone to his ear. "Well?"

"'Thriller'?"

"What? You don't know it?"

"Of *course* I know it—*everyone* knows it! It was number one all last year—how could I not know it?"

"So, what? You don't like it? You think people are tired of hearing it?"

"No, I think it's really cool—it's kind of a story, right? So we can act it out with our dancing."

"Like a horror story!"

"Right!"

Now they were both excited. Derek was up and pacing. Ideas for dance moves came into his mind, one after another.

"Okay, let me get a pen and paper so we can sketch out the routine," Vijay said. "You can play it line by line, and we'll pause it and figure out what we're doing."

An hour later, they had a basic outline of their dance: Two sixth-grade friends foolishly enter the local haunted house only to have the daylights scared out of them by a real-life monster, who emerges from the shadows and chases them away.

"Good work, partner!" Vijay said. "We have a killer song, a great story, and two fantastic, world-class dancers! We are going to win this talent show for sure!"

Derek laughed. He didn't know about winning the talent show—although that would be great if it happened. But he had his doubts. There were some super-talented kids at Saint Augustine's, and most of them had been practicing their skills for years. The competition was going to be fierce.

But he didn't say that to Vijay. After all, what was the point of being in a contest if you weren't going to try all out to win?

"I feel so much better now," Vijay admitted. "I was afraid for a minute there that you were going to chicken out on me."

"No way!" Derek protested. "When I said I wanted to do this, I meant it. We are good to go! And don't worry—after all this other stuff is out of the way, we're going to work this thing until we've got it totally down."

"Good!" Vijay said. "There's just one other small problem."

"Yeah? What's that?"

"Who are we going to get to play the part of the monster?"

Yikes. Derek hadn't thought of that.

"Never mind—we can figure that part out later," he told Vijay. "Just leave that job to me."

Chapter Seven
TESTING TIME

The week flew by, yet it seemed to take *forever*.

Every moment of Derek's life was taken up with school, sleep, study, homework, eating, or practicing basketball—sometimes more than one of them at a time!

Sam was trying his best, but there was no doubt that tutoring him—which was what Derek was pretty much doing—was slowing Derek's own studying down. On the other hand, going over things so thoroughly for Sam's sake did make Derek understand them better. So it wasn't a total waste of time, really—it just *felt* like it.

Derek and Vijay had touched base a bunch of times during the week. Vijay had not lost his enthusiasm for their project. In fact, ever since Derek had come up with their song, Vijay had been imagining how the dance/story would play out.

"I have choreographed practically the whole thing!" he told Derek that Thursday. "Don't have any worries—we are surely going to win first prize!"

Derek wasn't sure exactly what Vijay had cooked up. But he had to go along with it. There wasn't time for him to have any input—at least not yet.

All this had made the week fly by. It was Derek's *impatience* that made it feel endless. He couldn't stand waiting any longer—the sooner tryouts started, the sooner he would know whether he'd made the cut.

And now, it was Saturday at last! Here he was, getting out of the car with the basketball that hadn't left his hands all week, except in bed and in class and while he was studying with Sam. His left hand—his whole left arm—was tired and a little sore from all the dribbling.

Derek went inside the Y, headed for the gym. His dad drove on into the parking lot to find a spot.

In the gym Derek spotted Sam with his mom. She looked anxious, constantly checking her watch. Derek knew she was more concerned about Sam's grades than his hoop dreams. He wondered whether she was more worried Sam would *make* the team, or that he *wouldn't*.

"Derek! Hi!" Sam called, waving. Derek waved back but didn't go over there. Instead, he went into the gym, looking for Dave, with whom he'd been practicing for the past three days.

There was a confident look in his eyes, Derek noticed. Dave's game had come a long way, thanks to their coaching sessions with Derek's dad.

"You ready?" he asked as they exchanged their usual elaborate handshake.

"Ready as I'll ever be. You?"

"Now or never."

"Right. Good luck, man."

"You too."

Derek sure hoped they *both* made it. He knew he would feel bad if he made it and Dave didn't.

He didn't even want to think about the opposite result.

Mr. Jeter came into the gym and found a seat in the bleachers just as Coach Nelson blew his whistle for try-outs to get started.

Derek felt an incredible surge of energy course through his body. He kept hopping up and down, eager to get going. Looking around at all the other hopefuls, he saw that Dave was one of the tallest kids there. That would be a big advantage for him.

And what would be his own advantage? His speed? Maybe, but there looked to be plenty of fast-dribbling would-be point guards here.

Derek remembered what his dad had told him. "You might not be the most talented kid trying out. But you can make sure you *outwork* everybody else."

From the beginning, it was clear there weren't many slackers trying out. Everybody knew this was a competitive league, and it seemed like that had kept any so-so players at home.

There were fifteen spots on the team—three players at each position—and Derek could see that there were easily fifty kids there in the gym—probably even sixty.

Derek's energy kept threatening to overflow as he paced back and forth and hopped up and down, waiting for his turn to get on the court.

The coaches began by dividing the boys into groups of ten. Derek and Sam were put into the same group, and Dave in another. Derek wished it were the other way around. He did not relish the thought of having to go directly up against Sam. He wished Sam the best, but if only one of them was going to make the team at point guard, Derek didn't want to be the odd man out.

"Okay, kids," said Coach Nelson as everyone came to attention and stopped chattering. "We, um, well, I have to admit, more of you showed up than we expected. So my apologies to those of you who are going to have to wait a little while, but we can only handle three groups at a time. All right? Let's go!"

There were murmurs from the kids and concerned looks from their parents, who began checking their watches. But really, what could anyone do? There were only three coaches, and the gym was packed with kids wanting to try out.

"First group, go with Coach O'Neill. Second group"— this was Dave's group—"you're with Coach Bernstein.

Group three, you're with me. Groups four through six, hang out here awhile. We'll get to you in a few minutes."

So Derek, who was in group four, had to sit there, along with Sam and about thirty others, watching the first groups do drills.

It was pure torture. Derek was so full of nervous energy that he felt like it was going to overwhelm him, like a giant wave. Pretty soon he found himself unable to sit at all. He popped up like a piece of toast and began pacing around in front of the bleachers.

He wasn't the only one, either. It's hard to wait when you're primed for action—especially when people are going to be judging you on your performance!

Derek watched impatiently as Dave, Sam, and the others were put through a series of drills by the coaches. Dave and Sam's group started with layups, taking their turn in line before running toward the hoop and taking the bounce pass from the coach.

When they were done with layups—after tossing up five or six shots each—they switched over to Coach Nelson, who had them running up and down the court doing suicide sprints till they were ready to drop. Then they were sent to the other end of the gym, where they had to take shots from various points on the court, including free throws from the line.

Finally, the three groups took a seat, and groups four through six were finally called. With a quick wave to his dad, who gave him two thumbs up, Derek joined the other kids gathered around Coach Nelson.

As they got ready for their first set of sprints, Derek snuck a quick glance across at Sam—but Sam was busy concentrating and didn't notice. If he was feeling the heat from Derek's being there, he sure wasn't showing it.

Derek knew that Sam was the only kid he'd ever played ball with who was faster than he was. And sure enough, while Derek ran plenty fast enough to impress Coach Nelson, Sam edged him out every single time.

"Okay, boys, good job," said Coach Nelson when they were bent double and breathing hard and deep. "Head on over there to Coach O'Neill."

Derek had been practicing layups all week long. *Just sink the first one*, he told himself as he waited in line for his turn. *Don't try anything fancy. Not yet.*

He took off toward the basket, took the pass in stride, and laid it in as if he could have done it in his sleep.

"Attaboy!" said Coach O'Neal. "Next!"

Derek nailed his first three, then used his next three tries to show something extra. He drove left-handed and laid it in. Then he did a reverse layup from the right side. And on his final drive, he did a quick spin before laying it in with his left hand!

Derek was proud of himself. On this element at least, he'd posted a high bar for his competition to beat. And though Sam had nailed all his righty layups, he'd struggled from the left side, missing both times.

It wasn't that Derek was happy about it—Sam was his friend, after all, and Derek really did like him. But this was a competition. And he knew there might not be room on the team for both of them.

"Okay, men," said Coach O'Neill. "Go and check in with Coach Bernstein."

Derek had always been a pretty good shooter. But after Sam swished three incredible shots, Derek's confidence began to falter.

Between all that excess energy and the pressure Sam was putting on him, Derek found himself clunking shots he usually made. His aim was as true as ever, but every shot had either too much or too little behind it.

By contrast, Sam's shooting stroke showed no sign of wavering. He sank all seven shots he took, whispering "Yessss!" after each one and pumping his fist. Derek's shoulders slumped as he realized Sam was totally in his own happy zone. Not only was he not worried about Derek or anyone else as competition—he didn't even know anyone else existed!

They did another set of drills—five-man weave, set plays, running the court while passing back and forth—a lot of them the same ones Derek and Dave had practiced with Mr. Jeter.

Derek was in his element now, comfortable with the ball and accurate with his passes. He began to feel more confident again—but not enough to do any fist pumps. Not yet.

Groups four through six took their seats as the first three groups got up to do the second set of drills. After a further five-minute break for water and rest, the coaches lined all the boys up by position. Derek saw that there were eight other kids—including Sam—trying out for point guard. *Yikes.*

By contrast, there were only five kids vying for center, and Dave—lucky him—was one of them. The less competition, the better chance of making the team.

"We're going to have some scrimmages now," said Coach Nelson. "Two courts, four teams of twelve guys each. Everyone will get a turn, so be patient if you're not in the starting lineup. It's no reflection on how you're doing so far."

Derek and Dave wound up on opposing teams. "Good luck," they told each other before heading to their separate benches. Both boys knew that how they did here would tell whether they made the cut or not.

Derek was second in line to play point guard for his team. By the time he entered the scrimmage, the score was 10–4 in Dave's team's favor. Derek quickly moved the ball up the court, drove to his left, and dished off to one of the forwards for an open bucket.

"Nice! Nice!" Coach Nelson yelled, applauding. Derek felt his heart swell with happiness. Coach had noticed him!

But in that very second, the point guard for the other team blew past Derek and sank an easy layup. *Dang!*

Derek wasted no time in making up for his mistake. He protected the ball, drawing a double-team, then dished off to the center and rolled toward the basket. The center hit him as he went airborne, and Derek sank the layup—left-handed!

Without a second's pause, he ran back upcourt, just in time to foil a fast break by the other team. He dived at the other point guard from behind and knocked the ball away—straight to his own power forward!

Derek had skinned his right knee sliding on the polished wood floor. But he didn't mind that it was smarting a little. He knew his effort wouldn't go unnoticed.

Over the course of the next ten minutes, he sank another layup, had two more takeaways on defense, and took excellent care of the ball.

On the other hand, his shooting touch stayed cold—he wound up 1 for 5, and had two shots blocked—by Dave, of all people, who was putting in a really good showing on defense.

When Derek's replacement took over for him, his team had cut the deficit to two points. Dave remained in the game for his team the whole time, since he was their only center.

Coach Nelson gathered everyone in the bleachers when both scrimmages had ended. "Good job, everyone. You boys all gave it your best. Now Coach O'Neill and Coach

Bernstein and I will huddle up and decide who makes it to the next round. Check the bulletin board out front here on Monday afternoon to see if you're on the list. Final tryouts are same time next Saturday. So I'll see some of you then. If you're not on the list, thanks for coming out today—and try again next season."

Everyone clapped, and Derek went over to where Dave was standing. "Good job, man," he said sincerely. "You're definitely going to make it."

"Thanks!" Dave said, a big grin on his face. "You think so?"

"Definitely. You stuffed me twice, you dog!"

"Sorry. Doing my job."

"Totally. That's why I say you made it."

"Yeah. Well, you too!"

"Aw, I don't know . . . ," Derek said, shaking his head. "A lot of competition." He couldn't help looking over to where Sam was standing. "A *lot*."

"No worries," Dave said. "You were awesome!"

"Well, see you at school, I guess."

"Yeah. Testing time," said Dave. "You ready?"

"I guess," said Derek, again looking Sam's way. "You?"

"I've been pounding away at it. Nothing else to do except get ready for today."

Dave, of course, wasn't planning on being in the talent show. That's why he hadn't been under the kind of pressure Derek had been.

"Hey," said Derek, getting an idea. "I don't suppose you'd be willing to do a small part in Vijay's and my routine? Nothing big, just—"

"*No way!*" Dave said, putting both hands up. "Don't even think about it. I'd never get up in front of everybody and dance. Every time I've ever tried to, I got total stage fright!"

"You can't be afraid to fail, Dave! If you don't even try, you've already failed!"

Derek knew it was true—at least in his head. But what he didn't say was that he *himself* was nervous about getting up there. The only people he'd ever break-danced in front of were his family and Vijay—certainly not the whole school!

"Derek, you're my best friend—I would do anything for you, man. Just not this."

"But—" Derek sighed, giving up. "Okay. I just thought I'd ask."

"Sorry. I hate to let you down. I feel bad."

"You do?"

"Yeah . . . but not *that* bad." Dave said good-bye and went back to where his dad was waiting.

Too bad, thought Derek, watching him go. *He would have made a great monster.*

When he told Vijay he would find someone to play the monster, Derek didn't think it would be so hard to do. In the back of his mind, he'd figured he could always get Dave to do it.

But Dave's reaction didn't totally surprise him. Lots of people—especially shy ones—got stage fright. He would not have been in the talent show himself if he'd had to get up there and give a *speech*. Dancing was one thing—he had some decent moves—but speaking was another!

The problem was, with Dave out of the picture, where was Derek going to find a monster?

"Hey, Jeter! It's D-day! Zero hour! You ready to do battle with The Great Par-Nell?"

Derek rolled his eyes. "Morning, Gary."

Gary rubbed his hands together with relish. "English today, math tomorrow, and when it's all over, you shall be defeated, and I shall be your final boss! Bwah-ha-ha-ha!" Gary burst out laughing.

"Seriously?" Derek said a little lamely. "Gary, why don't you just come back down to Planet Earth? I know it seems alien to you, but . . ."

"Face it, Jeter, you are toast. You can study from now until forever, and I'll still be smarter than you. There's no substitute for genius."

Genius?

Gary's casual use of the word suddenly gave Derek a genius idea!

"So wrong," Derek said, a sly smile on his lips. "So very, very wrong."

"Ha!"

"Shall we make a little bet?"

"Okay, Einstein," Gary said, swallowing the bait. "You've got yourself a bet. If I beat you on the tests—no, *when* I beat you—I'm going to make you a T-shirt that says 'Gary P. Is Smarter than Me.' And you are gonna wear it. To *school*."

"And if *I* beat *you*," Derek said, "you have to be part of Vijay's and my talent show dance!"

"Ha! No way!" said Gary, smirking. "There's nothing lamer than a talent show—other than sports, of course."

"What's the matter, Gar?" Derek said. "Afraid of getting beat on the tests?"

"Are you nuts? There's no chance of that happening!"

"Then what are you worried about?"

Gary was cornered, and he knew it. "Okay, Mr. Talent—you're on! Highest total score wins. You lose."

The two boys shook on it.

Just then, Ms. Terrapin walked into the room, holding a stack of booklets. "Testing time!" she chirped, and all the students sat down at their desks.

Chapter Eight

RESULTS

"Dad? Can I go with you?"

Derek's father cocked his head to one side. "Don't you need to do math review? Remember, if you come along, you have to stay for Sharlee's whole dance class."

"That's okay," Derek assured him. "I'll bring my math book with me."

"I guess that'll be all right, then," said his dad. "I know the suspense must be killing you."

"You got that right!" Derek said with a laugh. He couldn't stand not knowing whether he'd made the cut for the next round of tryouts. Not when the list was already posted on the bulletin board at the Y!

He didn't want to hear it from Dave over the phone.

Derek knew that Chase would have driven him over there straight from school. If he stayed home, the phone would ring any minute, and it would be Dave, who would give him the news secondhand.

Besides, Derek wanted to know who else had made it through the first round. That would tell him who his competition was in the next round—if he got that far.

Although he liked dancing and was good at it, dance class would never have been Derek's thing. Plus, this was something called "jazz dance." Derek had no idea what that even meant—he guessed he'd find out now, sitting there watching Sharlee and the other kids.

At any rate, it would please Sharlee that he was coming to one of her activities. "I'll go get my book," he told his dad.

"Are you going to come to my recital next month?" Sharlee asked on the drive, her eyes wide with hope.

"Of course!" Derek assured her. "Would I miss something that fantastic?"

"It *will* be!" Sharlee said. "You can sit in the front row, because I have a big solo!"

"Wow!" said Derek. "That's so cool, Sharlee! Hey—don't you ever get scared, getting up and performing in front of people?"

"No," Sharlee said matter-of-factly. "Why would I do that?"

Derek laughed and shook his head. He tried to

remember if he'd been that sure of himself back when he was her age.

At any rate, it was pretty inspiring. If Sharlee could shake off any doubts about herself and her abilities, he figured he ought to be able to do the same.

"Well, I can't wait to see you up there, kickin' it," he said, giving her hand a squeeze.

Dancing was only one of Sharlee's many dreams—she wanted to be a soccer player, a black belt in karate, and a thousand other things. But Derek knew that she cared just as much about each of her dreams as he did about his. And that family and friends helped each other's dreams come true.

No sooner had they gotten to the Y than Derek took off at a run. "See you in class!" he told his dad and sister. He couldn't wait any longer, running at full speed until he made it to the bulletin board.

There was the notice.

Derek's heart was pounding—more from suspense than from running in from the parking lot.

There was his name! He'd made the cut!

"*YESSS*!" he cried out—then put his hand over his mouth, realizing that he was standing in a crowded lobby.

There was Dave's name too—right at the top of the list of centers!

This time Derek said "Yesss!" under his breath.

Of course, that meant another week of drilling, in

advance of the next round of tryouts. And this time he really would have to spend time with Vijay, preparing for the talent show.

Well, at least tonight was the last night of test prep—that would free up some hours—unless, of course, Ms. Terrapin had some other awful project up her sleeve.

Derek scanned the list more closely. The kids were listed by position. There were five centers, ten forwards for two positions, and twelve kids listed under guards. The name at the top of the guards list was Sam.

No surprise there. Of course, if Sam didn't score well enough on the big tests, his mom wouldn't let him play on the team.

Sam really cared about basketball. If he didn't get to play, it would be a crushing blow. It meant so much to him. . . .

"I hope he makes it," Derek murmured under his breath. "Even if it means I don't."

Even as he said the words, Derek wasn't really sure he meant them. Part of him did, anyway.

Of course, there was still room for them both. Derek wondered if the order in which they were listed meant anything. . . . Was it a ranking? Or was it just random . . . ?

He shook his head, not wanting to think about it anymore. He would just have to wait and find out, like all the rest of them. For now, at least, Derek felt relieved and happy. His and Dave's dream of playing basketball together was alive and well.

He slipped into the dance classroom as quietly as he could. The teacher was counting out beats, while two rows of six girls apiece went through their routine under her gaze.

In the middle of the front row stood Sharlee, who smiled and waved. Derek waved back, sat down next to his dad, and pulled out his math book.

It was hard to study, though, because he had to keep looking up every few seconds. Sharlee expected him to pay attention to what she was doing, and he didn't want to disappoint her. Besides, she really was kind of fun to watch.

In fact, at the moment, while the students were on a two-minute break, Sharlee was doing something that caught Derek's attention in a totally different kind of way. She seemed to be standing still while gliding to her left using only her feet—zigzagging from heel to toe and back again.

It was a move he'd seen a few times in music videos. It was funky and cool. Most important, it was perfect for his and Vijay's haunted house scenario!

Derek could see it playing out in his head—the two kids sneak along the walls of the house, doing that zigzag thing. Then when the monster comes out, they moonwalk away—getting nowhere while he gains on them!

Ka-ching! Derek pumped his fist in triumph. Vijay was going to totally love it!

"Thanks, Sharlee!" Derek told her as they buckled up in the backseat after class was over. "That was really fun. Educational, even!"

Sharlee beamed. "So can you come to my karate class tomorrow?"

"Ah, sorry," Derek said. "I've got to work with Vijay. But I think I learned a few dance moves today, thanks to you."

"Yay!"

"In fact, there's one of your moves I wish you would teach me. It's way cool."

"Which one?"

"That thing you do with the feet, like you're moving but you're not moving?"

"Oh—sure! It's easy. You'll see."

"You know, you've got the stuff."

"Huh?"

"Never mind. You just keep on doing whatever you're doing." He took her hand and held it the whole way home. Even though he got annoyed at her once in a while, Derek knew he had the greatest sister ever.

Derek looked back over his shoulder. Gary was grinning an evil grin at him, pencil in hand. As Derek watched, Gary put down the pencil, closed his test booklet, and got up to leave.

Derek frowned and looked over his other shoulder. There was Sam, beads of sweat glistening on his forehead as he tried to keep plowing through the math portion of the test.

Poor guy, thought Derek. *I hope he remembers at least some of what we went over. . . .*

"Eyes on papers, class!" Ms. Terrapin said, and Derek's neck swiveled back around so quickly that he felt a momentary twinge of pain as he focused back onto his test paper.

He didn't have much time to finish. It had been the same way yesterday. Derek was usually pretty quick at finishing tests, but not this time. It was harder for him to concentrate than usual. Other things kept intruding on his brain.

Yesterday it had been whether he'd made the cut for the team. Today it was next Saturday's final tryouts, plus the talent show. . . .

Derek forced all those other thoughts out of his mind. He got back to work, determined to focus on beating Gary.

"Nice moves!" Vijay said, clapping. "I love the worm! Can you teach me that one?"

"Sure!" The two boys were really into their work—making up for all that lost time.

This is really, really fun! Derek thought. It was the first time he'd felt the same excitement as Vijay about the talent show.

"I have to get home for supper," Vijay said. "Let's pick it up again tomorrow."

"Um, it's going to have to wait, Vij. I'm practicing basketball with Dave and my dad the next two days. It's the only time my dad can coach us."

"Oh." Vijay looked crestfallen. "But I thought after the tests, you—"

"Yeah, but . . . it winds up there's a second round of tryouts. Don't worry, though. It's over on Saturday, for keeps. Either I make the team or I don't—and even if I do, they only play on weekends, so it won't interfere."

Vijay sighed. "I guess it will be okay. We made good progress today in just one hour—so maybe that's how it will be next time too. I hope so."

They exchanged handshakes, and Vijay picked up his book bag. "Oh, by the way—who did you get to dance the part of the monster?"

Derek felt his stomach drop. *Oops.*

"It's . . . a surprise—I'll tell you tomorrow. But I think you'll be pleased."

"Like with the song, huh? Cool," said Vijay, and headed out the door. "I love surprises. See you in class tomorrow!"

Derek slumped into a chair. Boy, he sure hoped he beat Gary out on the tests. If not, there was no plan B.

And what would he tell Vijay then?

• • •

"Class—thanks to Scantron technology, we have your practice test results back already!"

A rumble of anxious conversation arose from the room. Ms. Terrapin clapped her hands for quiet. "You can feel free to share your scores with one another, or not. However, there are three of you with whom I will speak privately after class, about getting extra help after school between now and the real tests next spring."

Derek looked over at Sam, whose head was hanging down and shaking slowly from side to side.

Ms. Terrapin walked slowly up and down the aisles, placing a single folded sheet of paper on each student's desk. Derek held his breath as she placed his sheet in front of him. He tried to swallow, but his mouth was too dry.

He unfolded the paper slowly and peeked inside. There were three grades:

English: 675

Math: 724

Total: 1399

Derek took in a deep breath, his eyes wide. A 1399! That was much higher than he'd imagined he'd get! It made him think he had a real chance of beating out Gary's score.

Speaking of Gary, here he was now, leaning over Derek's shoulder. "Well?" he asked.

"You first," Derek said, trying again to swallow, with the same result.

"Read it and weep, Je-Ter." He dangled his paper for Derek to read.

Derek gasped in happy surprise. Gary's grades were:

English: 692

Math: 706

Total: 1398

"I win!" Derek cried, getting up and thrusting both arms in the air. "Check it out, Par-Nell! *1399!*"

Gary stared at Derek's grades, dumbfounded. "This has got to be a misprint," he said, shaking his head. "There's no way! It can't be right!"

"That's what happens when you don't study," Derek said, trying not to rub it in too much. "Nobody told you to chuck the booklet and play computer games the whole time."

"I underestimated you, Jeter," Gary said, losing the robot voice. "You must have spent every waking minute cracking the books. That's the only way you could possibly have come close, let alone come out ahead."

"Oh well," Derek said with a shrug and a smile. "I guess you can try again in the spring. Meanwhile, we had a bet. And now, it's time to pay up—*Mr. Monster.*"

"Huh?"

Derek chuckled. "You'll see. Don't worry—you're going to be the star of the show!"

"Omigosh! *Gary Parnell?*"

"That's right," Derek said. "I got him good, too."

"This is great news, Derek! He will be the perfect monster. And the worse he dances, the better for our story—it is a no-lose situation!"

"I told you I'd get someone," Derek said with a grin.

"Still, it must have been difficult—I mean, Gary, of all people! Who would have thought he would agree to do such a thing?"

"Yeah," Derek agreed, folding his arms across his chest in satisfaction. "Who would have thought it?"

Chapter Nine

PAIN IN THE NECK

"Show me again how you do it, Sharlee."

Sharlee clucked her tongue and rolled her eyes. "Derek, I already showed you a million times! It's so easy!"

"You showed me exactly twice. But never mind, just show me one more time. Please?"

He gave her a quick tickle under her arm, and she squealed with laughter. "Okay, okay! Stop!"

"Now, here we go," said Derek, getting in position. "Stand next to me so I can do it like you."

"Okay—so if you're going left, you put your weight on your left heel and your right toe. Got that?"

"Okay, now what?"

"You swivel on your left heel, and turn the toe out to the

left. At the same time, you move your right heel to the left, pivoting on the toe. Then you just keep switching, in and out—like this. It's *easy*!"

"Sheesh," Derek said, making an awkward attempt as Sharlee glided effortlessly to the left. "Wow, Sharlee, you sure are a good dancer."

"You can do it, Derek! Just keep practicing. But I have to go now. Daddy's taking me over to Ciara's for a play date."

She ran out of the living room, calling, "Daaad! We have to go!"

Derek blew out a breath and tried the move again—slowly. Eventually, he got the hang of it. When he was done, he went on to perfect his moonwalking.

It was almost four—Vijay was due over any minute now. They were going to finally get down to planning out their dance routine. Now that Gary was roped into being part of it, Derek and Vijay could map things out, knowing they had a monster lined up.

When Vijay arrived the two friends set to work. "Okay, should we start with the story?" he asked Derek. "Or should we go through all the moves we know first?"

"Let's get the story down," Derek said. "Then we'll know what kind of moves we need to get it across."

"Okay. Sounds good. So from what we talked about on the phone, I have fleshed it out a lot. So let's start with the basics, all right? Two friends"—he pointed to himself and Derek—"each thinks he's braver than the other. So they dare each other to go into the haunted house. We can do that with dance moves, like trying to outdo each other."

"What are we going to do to show the house?" Derek wondered. "Is the audience just going to have to imagine it?"

Vijay thought for a moment. "I'll paint a big poster of a house—maybe even with the words 'Haunted—Do Not Enter!'—and we can hang it from the back curtain."

"Sounds good, but—"

"Don't worry, I know you're busy with basketball and such. I'll do the poster."

"Cool. So what next?"

"So then we do all our fancy walking moves, edging closer and closer to the house, right? Moving in, backing off, 'cause we're really scared underneath. Then finally we get there, and we're about to go in when the monster comes out and tries to get us!"

"That's when we can do our floor moves—spins and flips—"

"And that worm thing you do!" Vijay said. "And at the end, when the monster talks? We try to get away, but he keeps getting closer, and closer—'cause we're moonwalking, and we're not getting anywhere!"

Both boys cracked up, and Derek applauded. "Good job, Vij!" he said. "Man, you've done a lot of good work on this!"

"Oh, it's nothing," he said, waving Derek off. "When I

get excited, all kinds of ideas come into my head."

"That's for sure." Derek clapped his hands together. "So why don't we put the song on and go line by line, figuring out what moves to do?"

They got about halfway through, then sat down to write down everything in an outline form, so they wouldn't forget all the details.

"Okay, we can pick this up tomorrow," Vijay said.

Derek was about to suggest they put it off till after the tryouts on Saturday—but he just couldn't disappoint Vijay yet again. He'd already put him off so many times. And besides, this routine was looking like it was actually going to be good!

Derek knew Vijay was right—it was going to take practice. They each had some good moves, but the story demanded that they do a bunch of things in unison, and that meant they would have to learn each other's moves.

"See you tomorrow," he told his friend.

"See you tomorrow, Derek. Hey, by the time we get to the talent show, we will be ready for prime time! Watch out world, here we come!"

"Tell me again why I have to do this?"

"We made a bet, Gary," Derek said. "And I won!"

Gary rolled his eyes. "Whatever." He heaved a sigh. "So what do I have to do?"

"Not all that much, really."

The two boys were standing in the hallway after school. Lots of kids were passing by, and Derek didn't want to reveal anything about their act to anyone. He wanted it to be a surprise when they got up there onstage—especially Gary's appearance in the dance. His name, at his own request, would not appear in the program for the show.

"Still, I suppose I have to actually rehearse for this pathetic excuse of an act?"

"Yes, you will. But like I say, don't panic. All you have to do is make like Frankenstein and move your mouth when the monster in the song says his piece."

"This is so *juvenile*," Gary protested.

"Nuh-uh-uh!" Derek said, wagging his index finger at Gary. "Don't even get started, dude. I beat you, fair and square."

"Don't remind me."

"It'll be next week sometime," Derek said. "Probably early in the week. Keep your afternoons free—it'll be at my house. You know where that is?"

"No, but I'm sure you'll tell me," said Gary miserably. "Ugh. This is going to be even worse than being forced to play baseball last spring."

"Ah, be quiet—you loved it, and you know it."

"That is ridiculous," Gary said.

But Derek knew it was true, even though Gary would never admit it. Hopefully, he'd get over being in the talent show too.

Derek was on his way out of the building when Sam came up behind him. "Hey!" he said, flashing a big smile. "Guess what?"

"You passed?"

"Yesss! Thanks to you, buddy! I would have never gotten there without you!"

"Ah, come on, I'm sure you would have."

"I passed by *four points*, Derek. *Four. Points.* There's no way I could have done it without you. Just think—now my mom will let me be on the under-twelve team!"

"Yeah! That's . . . great!"

Derek hoped he sounded more excited than he really felt. Sam was definitely going to make the basketball team. That left only two slots at point guard, with twelve kids called back at guard for Saturday.

Derek still had a chance to make the team, but it had just gone down by a lot.

In spite of the fact that they'd only had one hour to rehearse today, the routine was coming along. Derek and Vijay had already choreographed most of the song. There were a few gaps where they both agreed they needed to find new moves to cover. But for that, they'd have to watch some music videos for research. As for the monster's part, it would have to wait until Gary was there.

The two boys spent the rest of their time teaching each other their moves. They promised each other to have them down by next week's rehearsal, so they could try them out in unison to the music.

After Vijay was gone, Derek continued to practice the moves his friend had taught him. There was the sphinx-like head move, with the chin jutting out then in, and the side-to-side head shift, left to right and back again without tilting the head. There were the arm waves, like swimming—Vijay had picked those moves up at the family wedding in India. And there was this wobbly leg thing Vijay did that was really good for showing how scared they were of the monster.

Derek finished off his practice session by doing some more worms, twists, and anything else he could do in the family's small living room, which had the most open space of any room in the house. Things like cartwheels and such would have to wait till they had a bigger space to practice in.

"Derek? Dinner is ready!" his mom's voice called out from the kitchen. "Everyone else is at the table. Are you coming?"

"Be right there, Mom!" He put away the CD and washed his hands, then joined the rest of the family at the table.

He went to bed that night feeling tired and a bit sore. He hoped he hadn't overdone it. But there was always tomorrow to rest up and get ready for Saturday morning's big tryout.

He was excited about the talent show, too—for sure.

But he was twice as excited about making the basketball team!

And ten times as nervous that he wouldn't.

"OW!! Ow! Ow! Ow!"

Derek shot up in bed. The pain in his neck was sharp and intense. Every time he tried to move it to the right or forward, the pain shot through him and made him cry out in agony.

No, no, nononono—this cannot be happening! he thought, a wave of panic coming over him.

He must have twisted it last night, doing some of those new moves! But it hadn't bothered him at the time.

Then he thought back to Tuesday, when Ms. Terrapin's sharp rebuke had caused him to twist his neck around. He'd been looking back at Gary and Sam, he remembered, and the quick maneuver had caused that same spot in his neck to hurt for just a second.

He wondered now if that could have caused this. Or maybe it was one thing on top of the other . . . ?

It hardly mattered now. Basketball tryouts were just twenty-four hours away! How was he going to recover in time?

"Mom!" he called out. "MOM!!"

She came running up the stairs. "What is it, old man? Are you okay?"

"I can't move my neck!"

He proceeded to explain how he might have injured it.

She examined him closely. "You need to have the school nurse look at it—she'll know better than I do—but it sounds like you pulled or strained a muscle, and now it's seizing up with spasms."

"Spasms?" It sounded terrible!

"Your dad and I have both had them before. They usually go away after a couple of days."

"*A couple of days?*" Derek repeated. "It has to be better by *tomorrow*! I've got basketball tryouts!"

"Well, if it isn't, you'll have to explain to the coach."

"Mom, no! He won't understand—I'll never get on the team if I can't play!"

"Let's just see what happens," said his mom. "Maybe you'll feel better by then."

"I *have* to try out—no matter what!"

"Derek, if you play with an injury you might hurt yourself even worse. If it isn't mostly gone by tomorrow morning, you'll have to accept the reality of the situation and explain things to the coach."

Derek started to slump but jerked back with a wince as the pain kicked in again.

"Look, let's get you ready for school now. Otherwise you'll be late."

"School?! *I can't even move!*"

"I'll drive you there on my way to work. We'll put some ointment on it—that should help. You'll just have to take it slow and easy today. These things are usually at their worst in the morning."

Derek couldn't see how he could possibly be all better by tomorrow. He could try to play with some pain, but he knew it would affect his game—not to mention that he might wind up making his neck worse!

After all that dreaming with Dave . . . he was now facing the worst possible scenario: Dave making the team and him being left out—just because of a freak injury at the very last minute!

Why couldn't this have happened next week—or next *month*? Why did it have to happen *now*—at the worst possible moment?

Chapter Ten

DISASTER!

"What do you mean, you can't move?!"

Derek didn't answer right away. What could he say? What could he tell Vijay to make him not freak out?

"I just . . . it hurts if I turn my neck."

"What are we going to do now? How can we practice?" Vijay looked forlorn and defeated.

Derek tried to nod, but had to stop, wincing in pain. He sympathized with his friend—after all, he was excited about their dance too—but Derek had other, more urgent problems of his own.

"Look, Vij," he said. "The talent show's still two weeks away. The school nurse and my mom both said this should be better in a few days."

"I hope so," Vijay said dejectedly. "Because if not, this whole thing is going to be a total disaster."

Derek watched his friend shuffle slowly down the hallway, past the kids at their lockers getting ready to go home for the weekend. Vijay was usually so upbeat—so positive about everything. Derek had rarely seen him this down.

Derek's dad picked him up from school, so that he'd be more comfortable than on the bus. When they got home, Derek put some of his mom's wintergreen ointment on his neck, and a heating pad for good measure. It was starting to feel better, and everything he did to treat it helped a little more. Derek was starting to think there was a glimmer of a chance he could try out the next day.

By the time he went to bed that night, he was amazed at how much his neck had improved. The pain was less than half what it had been that morning!

Gazing up at the scoreboard, Derek saw that his team had a 1-point lead, with only thirty seconds left!

He drove the lane, feeding the ball off to Dave, who took the open 3-pointer—SWISH!

Derek flew back down the court on defense—but the other team's point guard went airborne, right over his head, and slammed home a ferocious dunk!

Hey—it was Sam Rockman, of all people! Wasn't he supposed to be on Derek's team?

No time to think about that—only fourteen seconds left! Derek took the inbounds pass and rushed the ball up the court, drawing the double-team. Again, he dished it off to Dave—but this time, Derek took off for the basket, and Dave fed him the pass in full flight. . . .

Derek was about to lay it up when a huge hand swatted the ball away!

Derek swung his head around to see who it was—

"OWWW!! OW! OW! OWWW!"

Tears welled up in his eyes as the pain shot through his neck. He must have aggravated it waking up from his dream!

Oh no! All his hopes of waking up with no pain were gone—out the window! He had to move as slowly as a turtle to get out of bed, wincing more than once when his neck moved too much.

"How is it?" said his mom, coming in to see what the noise was all about. "Oh. I see. Gee, that's too bad. Sorry, hon."

Derek felt the tears coming and fought them back with every fiber of his being. "I'm not going to tryouts!" he said bitterly.

"Of course you are, old man," she told him, gently rubbing the back of his neck. "We honor our commitments. And you've committed to being on this team."

"I can't bear just sitting there watching, Mom!"

"Of course you can. And of course you *will.* If you can't impress the coach with the quality of your play, you can at least impress him with the quality of your character and your commitment."

Derek sighed. He knew his mom was right. He would show up and tell the coach what had happened. He would sit there on the bench and root for Dave and Sam to make the team without him.

"Okay," he told his mom.

"I'll be right there with you the whole time," she assured him. "We'll see this through together. And try not to give up hope, old man. One thing your dad and I learned before we met, back when we were both in the military—when you show up for duty no matter what, amazing things can happen."

They got there half an hour early—before any of the other kids arrived. Coach Nelson was there, along with the two assistant coaches, going over their notes with one another, reviewing and comparing what they'd marked down about each kid who'd tried out.

"Don't be afraid, Derek—just tell Coach what happened and why you're here." His mother gave him a kiss on the forehead and a gentle pat on the shoulder. "I'll be right here." Then she took a seat in the bleachers.

Derek went up to the coach, who was busy writing in his notebook. "Sir?" he finally said. "Excuse me, but—"

"You're here early," said Coach Nelson. "What's your name again? Darrin something?"

"Derek, sir. Derek Jeter."

"I'm busy right now, Derek. You can get warmed up over in that area or just sit for a few minutes till the other kids get here."

"I . . . I can't try out today," Derek said haltingly.

"Huh? I don't understand."

"I hurt my neck the other day. It hurts when I move it a certain way." He sighed, feeling a lump rising in his throat. "I really, really want to be on the team," he said. "I just—can't play today."

"How did you wind up hurting yourself?" asked the coach.

"I was practicing."

He was going to leave it at that, but the coach asked, "For the team?"

"Not exactly," said Derek, looking down at the gym floor. "I'm in the school talent show with my friend, and we're doing a break dancing routine."

"Ouch," said the coach. "Rolling on your neck, twisting in corkscrews, that kind of thing?"

Derek nodded silently.

"Well, kid, thanks for being up front about it. I like that in my players. You're a real stand-up guy. You could have just called, but you came all the way down here to tell me in person. Too bad you're not able to play today—you looked good in that first round. I guess I'll see you next season." He offered his hand.

"Thanks," said Derek, shaking it as he looked down at his shoes.

So it was over, then. "See you next season," the coach had said. That meant Derek was *out* for *this* season.

He sat back down next to his mother. She threw an arm around him and let him lean his head on her shoulder. "Keep your chin up, old man," she whispered. "You did the right thing. You're *doing* the right thing."

The other players began to file in. Dave waved to Derek and smiled, then saw the look on his face and came over. "What's going on?" he asked.

"I can't do it," Derek said. "My neck's messed up."

"Wow. Seriously? That really stinks! Man, I can't believe this."

"Believe it," Derek said.

The coach blew his whistle. Dave said, "I'd better get over there. Sorry, Derek. Maybe it'll work out somehow." He shrugged, then turned to go.

"It won't," Derek said, mostly to himself.

But his mom heard him. "You don't *know* that, Derek," she said. "One thing you do know—you handled it as well as possible."

Derek and his mom watched as the kids went through their drills, then faced off in a full-court scrimmage. Dave and Sam both stood out at their positions—but all the kids were really good. Sitting there watching, Derek wasn't sure he'd have made the team anyway, even if he had been down there playing.

At the end of practice Coach Nelson and the assistant coaches gathered the boys together on the bleachers, across the gym from where Derek and his mom were sitting. He told them they'd done well and that the results would be posted the following Friday. He told the kids if they didn't make the team, it didn't mean they weren't good players. He encouraged them all to try again next season—the same thing he'd told Derek before tryouts began.

Then he dismissed the kids, and they began scattering, talking in groups as they looked for their rides home.

Derek watched them all go. Some were excited, feeling they'd played well enough to make the team. Others seemed less sure or even somewhat downcast.

At least those kids had been given a chance to prove themselves. He hadn't even had that!

Just as he was really feeling sorry for himself, he looked up and saw Coach Nelson staring at him from clear across the gym.

The coach walked slowly over to Derek and his mom, holding his notebook under his arm.

"I can't believe you're still here!" he said to Derek. "First in, last out, huh?" He turned to Mrs. Jeter. "I assume you're this young man's mom?"

"That's me," she said. "Dorothy Jeter."

"Paul Nelson. You ought to be mighty proud of your son. He's got the right work ethic."

"He's committed to making this team," she replied. "In our family, we don't take our commitments lightly."

"Not even to being in talent shows, I gather," said the coach with a bit of a grin.

"It's good to try all kinds of things," said Derek's mom.

"Yes, indeed, Mrs. Jeter." Coach Nelson cleared his throat. "Uh, listen—Derek, I have to say, you've made an impression on me today, tryout or no tryout. Coming in person instead of calling, getting here early—and staying the whole time, even though you must have been aching to get out there and play. That can't have been easy. . . ."

"No," Derek admitted. "It wasn't."

"Now, as you can understand, I have to pick my team from the kids who were on the floor today. And I can't schedule a private tryout, just for you."

Derek nodded. *Of course* he knew all that. What was the coach getting at?

"Normally, I wouldn't do this—but since I don't have to post the roster till Friday, I'm going to bend the procedures a little."

He sat down on Derek's other side. "I also coach the under-fourteen traveling team," he said. "They're going to be scrimmaging Thursday evening. If your neck is all better by then, you can come down here and I'll get you into the game. That'll stand as your tryout—if you're up for playing with kids who are older and more advanced, that is."

"Yesss! *Ow!!*" Tears came to Derek's eyes, finally—from the pain in his neck—but now they were tears of joy. He couldn't believe the coach was giving him another chance to make the team! "Thanks, Coach Nelson!"

"You earned yourself a second chance, kid," said the coach, clapping him on the shoulder—gently. "Character counts, at least with me. Let's just hope you're less clumsy on the court than you are on the dance floor."

They all laughed at that one. Then Nelson said, "Nice to meet you, Mrs. Jeter. Hope to see you both here on Thursday night."

"You will," said Derek's mom, "whether Derek can play by then or not, we'll be here."

"I'm *playing*! I'm *totally* playing!" Derek insisted. "Don't worry, Coach," he said. "These things almost always heal in a couple of days. Right, Mom?"

"Yikes. My exact words," she admitted. "Not that I'm a doctor. But let's hope so."

After the coach walked away, Derek hugged his mom fiercely. "Thanks, Mom," he said. "Thanks for coming with me today."

"You know your family will always be behind you, Derek," she said. "But *I* know you would have shown up here today anyway. For Dave, if for no other reason."

It was *true*. Derek hadn't thought of it—but the dream of playing on this team together belonged to *both* of them.

And now that dream was still alive!

"You're the best, Mom!" he said, hugging her. "Thanks. Thanks for everything."

Chapter Eleven
ON THE CLOCK

Yes, he felt better. Just knowing he still had a chance of making the team went a long way. Not only that, but his neck was definitely improving. He woke up Sunday and could actually move it around without wincing—although he was still treating it very gingerly.

On Monday and Tuesday after school, he and Vijay were able to go over their routine, with nothing else but regular old homework to distract them.

It was too bad Derek couldn't actually try any of his dance moves, but at least Vijay was able to work on getting his down. Derek coached him, and the results really showed. Vijay was going to blow some kids' minds when they saw him dance!

Derek also went through the whole sequence of moves in his head, memorizing them so that when he *could* dance again, he could just slip right into the routine.

He and Vijay had already agreed that Derek would give his neck a rest until the basketball scrimmage on Thursday evening. Starting Friday—exactly one week before the show—the two boys would start running through their whole number full out.

On Tuesday, Derek told Gary, "We need you to come over tomorrow and walk through your part."

"Ugh," Gary said. "*Torture*. But okay, I'll be there. *Not* because I *owe* you anything, Jeter—I just don't want to look bad up there." He shivered with disgust. "Enjoy your short-lived triumph, Jeter. Revenge is going to be sweet, next time I win."

"You brought this on yourself, Gary," Derek said coolly. "You could have studied for those tests like all the rest of us. You just thought you didn't need to."

"I underestimated you, it's true," Gary admitted. "*By one stinking point*. Next time I won't make that mistake."

Derek said nothing except, "See you tomorrow." There was no sense irritating Gary any further—not when they needed him to show up for their act.

"It's a pretty cool song, I have to admit." Gary sat in Derek's living room, arms folded across his chest. "Never heard it before."

"What planet have you been living on?" Vijay said, amazed. "It was number one for like fifty straight weeks this last year!"

"I don't listen to music," said Gary flatly. "It's a total waste of time."

"What *isn't*, according to you?" Vijay shot back as Derek cued up the song to the spot where Gary came onstage.

"Let's see . . . math . . . chess . . . computer games . . . eating . . . did I say math?"

"Okay, okay," Derek said. "Let's go through your part again, Gar."

Gary moaned, suffering with the effort of having to stand up and trudge over to the hall doorway for his entrance. "Do we have to? We've already done it twice."

"It's called *rehearsal*," Vijay said impatiently. "Practice makes perfect."

"Speak for yourself," said Gary drily. "Once is plenty for me. I'm always perfect the first time."

"Modest, too," quipped Derek. "Okay, here goes."

He pushed the play button and the music came on. As the voice spoke its ghoulish words, Gary walked stiffly into the room. He was wearing a black satin cape Vijay had brought over to use as a costume. Now he walked in like Frankenstein—stiff arms raised, hands bent like claws, mouth opening and shutting as if he was mechanically speaking along with the voice on the recording.

Then, on cue, he broke into something like a chicken

dance—except that Gary had a unique style of moving his body. The effect was funky, yet funny—in fact, it was *perfect*—just as Gary had said!

"Don't change a thing about it," Derek said, applauding when the music faded out and the dance was done. "Gary, you're a natural!"

"An *unnatural* natural!" Vijay chimed in.

"Ha! That's a good one," Gary said. "Okay, I'm done. See you onstage at the talent show, guys."

"Oh no." Derek stopped him. "You've got to show up a couple more times for run-throughs next week, when my neck is better and I can dance again."

"Don't push your luck with me, Jeter. Consider yourselves lucky I showed up once."

"You're on the hook, Gar," Derek reminded him. "A promise is a promise."

"Hmmm," said Gary. "Whatever. Right now I'm out of here—that's all I know."

"Don't worry, Gary," said Vijay as Gary headed for the door. "You are going to be a smash hit!"

"Yeah, right," said Gary. "We'll *all* be lucky if we're not the laughingstock of the whole school after this." He turned and left, shutting the front door behind him.

"Don't listen to him," Vijay said. "You saw what a hoot he was, dancing like that."

"He *was*, wasn't he? Let's just hope he doesn't decide to get creative and change things before the performance."

• • •

That evening the whole Jeter family drove to Westfield Dance Studios to watch Sharlee perform in the school's semiannual recital. Derek was in a good mood—glad to get his mind off things. For tonight, he could be nervous for his sister instead of himself.

As for Sharlee, she didn't seem the least bit anxious about performing in front of a crowd of people. She was her usual bubbly, talkative self, making them all laugh.

When she stepped out onstage with the rest of the dancers, her family stood up in the audience and clapped and whooped for her. She turned and waved, beaming her happiest smile. But in doing so, she fell out of rhythm with the other dancers.

Derek thought this little slipup might rattle his sister. But no—not Sharlee. Instead of checking the other kids to get back in sync with them, she kept right on with what she was doing.

And far from being tentative and halfway with her dance moves, she threw herself into it as if she were the only person on the stage!

The audience *loved* it—and not just her own family, either. At the end, when the dancers took their individual bows, Sharlee got the biggest ovation of them all!

Afterward, the Jeters went out for ice cream sundaes to celebrate. And none of them mentioned the fact that Sharlee had been out of rhythm.

So what if she'd done some little thing wrong? There was so much she'd done *right*!

This hit home to Derek as he sat there, fighting off ice-cream brain freeze. It wasn't being perfect that mattered; it was being *totally committed*.

Sharlee couldn't have pulled it off if she'd been afraid to fail! If even a brief moment of doubt had interrupted her flow, she wouldn't have succeeded in winning over the audience.

Derek stored this important nugget of wisdom away in the back of his brain. He knew it might come in handy— *and soon*.

For days now, Derek had been feeling more and more confident. Coach Nelson had given him renewed hope of making the team—and his neck was hardly bothering him at all!

On top of everything, his dance with Vijay was looking like a winner—especially now that Gary's fantastic monster bit had been added into the mix!

He'd seen how Sharlee had overcome a gaffe at the very beginning of her performance and gone on to steal the show. So Derek knew that if something went wrong during their "Thriller" routine, he could still overcome it.

And yet . . .

He lay in bed in the darkness, the same old fears beginning to creep back into his brain. He kept hearing Gary's mocking voice in his head, and it just would not shut up.

Tomorrow was Thursday—Derek's big chance to make the team. But to succeed, he'd have to impress the coach with more than just his character—against a team of older kids who'd already proven they were the best in town—good enough to be on the traveling team!

The more he thought about it, the more Derek realized he was going to have to up his game to another level. Dave and Sam had already made a great impression. But that was against kids their own age. Derek now faced a far more difficult test.

"Hey, old man. Still awake, huh?" His mom's head peeked around the bedroom door. "Want to talk about it?"

Derek sat up in bed, and she sat down next to him. "I can't sleep, Mom," he said. "I keep thinking about tomorrow night."

She put an arm around him. "It's going to be a big test for you, Derek, for sure. But you've had big tests before. You know you can ace them if you focus on bringing your very best. But you won't be able to do that if you don't get enough sleep."

"I just can't!" Derek moaned. "Every time I start to nod off, it comes back into my head!"

"Well, if it helps any, Dad and I have complete faith in you. Try picturing yourself already on the team, sinking baskets and stealing balls. That might help." She got up, tucked him back into bed, and kissed him on the forehead.

"In the meantime, just visualize yourself succeeding. Or even better—think about Sharlee. Nothing's ever going to stop her from being successful. Don't you let anything stop you, either."

Chapter Twelve

SHOWTIME!

What if I choke and miss all my shots?

What if I throw the ball away, trying to make a dazzling pass just to impress the coach?

What if I . . . ?

The closer they got to the Y, the greater Derek's dread grew. The pressure on him was enormous. In order to make the under-12 team, he had to do better than just hold his own with these older, more experienced players—he had to *stand out*.

When Dave had first mentioned trying out for the team together, Derek hadn't realized how much he really wanted to do it. Somehow, he'd just assumed it would be kind of fun.

He hadn't thought about how *competitive* the AAU league was—about how hard it might be to make the team in the first place.

And now Dave was *counting* on him.

Derek watched the windshield wipers go back and forth, back and forth, making their swishing, clicking sound. His heart beat in rhythm along with them as he sat in the backseat.

"How're you holding up, Derek?" his dad asked from the driver's seat without turning around.

"Fine," Derek said flatly.

"That's good," said Mr. Jeter. "Don't try to do too much, now. Just go out there and play your regular game, and you'll be okay."

Derek sighed and nodded. He'd heard all of it before— but *knowing* it wasn't the same as going out there and *doing* it.

Once again Derek was the first kid to arrive in the gym. Coach Nelson looked up and grinned. "I shouldn't be surprised," he said, coming over to shake hands. "Nice to meet you, Mr. Jeter. Mrs. Jeter, good to see you again. And you are . . . ?"

"Sharlee! I'm Derek's sister!"

"Well, nice to meet you, too, Sharlee."

"I can play basketball too!"

"I'll bet you can," said the coach with a smile. Then he turned to Derek. "You ready?"

"Uh-huh."

"How's the neck?"

Derek had to laugh. "It's good! Thanks for asking."

"Well, make yourselves comfortable. Here, Derek. Take this ball and put up a few shots while you're waiting."

Once the other kids arrived, the coaches formed them up into two teams for the scrimmage. The traveling team season was due to begin the following week, and this would serve as their final preparation.

So it was a surprise to them—and an *unpleasant* surprise to several—that some kid who wasn't even on the team was going to play in their scrimmage. A *younger* kid—an under-12!

There were several murmured comments and hard looks that Derek noticed. He hadn't even thought about that part of being here.

On the other hand, it didn't change a thing for him. He wasn't here to impress them—he was here to *outwork* them!

The scrimmage began with Derek on the bench. He watched as his team—in the yellow pinnies—took the jump ball from the blue pinnies and moved upcourt.

His team was just that—a team. The players knew exactly where to position themselves. They were executing a play they must have drilled in practice.

Now Derek had something else to worry about—how was he going to run the offense at point guard without knowing any of the plays?

Coach Nelson hadn't said a word to Derek about it. Yet the starting point guard had shouted out "Duke! Duke!" and right away, the forwards had set picks at either side of the foul line, and the center had moved under the basket. It was like clockwork.

The blueshirts did the same on offense. Both teams were using man-on-man defenses, so the game had a slow pace. There was no time clock, of course, so the guards did a lot of dribbling, looking for the open man to pass to—or else driving and dishing off when the double-team came.

Derek sat there, observing all this as the game went on. It was an intense scrimmage with plenty of personal fouls. Derek saw that ten minutes had run off the clock. Yet he'd been sitting on the bench for almost twenty.

He began to wonder when he would ever get his chance. Already, there had been a few substitutions by each team. Derek found himself nervously tapping his toes, drumming on his knees with his hands, getting antsier by the minute.

Finally, his turn came. The whistle blew for a two-shot foul on his team's point guard. After the opposing guard made the first shot, the assistant coaching Derek's team signaled for the offending point guard to come out. Then he pointed to Derek. "Go get 'em, kid," he said, clapping twice.

Derek didn't need a second invitation. He sprang off the bench like a coiled snake—all that pent-up energy coursing through him.

Calm down! he told himself. *Relax! It's just another game, remember? Don't try to do too much!*

The second foul shot was good, tying the game.

Derek ran all the right messages through his brain. But his body wanted to *go, go, go!* From the moment he took the inbounds pass, he was off and running.

Until now the pace of the game had been tortoise-like, and Derek had been going crazy on the bench. Now his boundless nervous energy took over. He raced right past two defenders and went airborne for the easy layup—

But the ball clanked off the rim! He'd given the shot too much energy, and blown it!

Derek felt the blood rush to his face as he ran back on defense. There was no time to think—his miss had given the other team a fast break. Derek flew down the court, leapt into the air, and with his fingertips outstretched, flicked the ball away from the unwary blueshirt who'd been just about to lay one up himself!

The assistant acting as referee blew his whistle and signaled that the ball belonged to the blue team. Still, Derek had managed to avert the worst—at least for the moment.

He scanned the court, watching the eyes of the kid throwing the ball in. Anticipating the pass, Derek moved in a flash, and stole it!

Again, he rushed upcourt, dribbling right past the surprised defenders. This time he pulled up for a quick jump shot.

But once again he'd put too much energy into it! The ball hit the backboard and bounced high off the rim.

Derek rushed to get the rebound, just as a blueshirt grabbed it. He wrapped his arms around the ball too, and the whistle blew.

"Jump ball!"

Derek now had to outjump a kid seven inches taller than he was. He tried to time it just right—and lo and behold, managed to tip it to one of his teammates!

So far, his play had been a mixed bag. He hadn't scored any points, even though he'd had two golden opportunities. On the other hand, he'd made three good defensive plays and shown that he could jump with any of them.

But now that the other kids had been alerted to his presence on the court, his teammates seemed to silently conspire to keep the ball away from him.

Time after time, Derek would get himself free on offense, call for the ball, only to be ignored. The ball holder would pass it to someone else who wasn't nearly as open. Or he would drive straight into a double-team rather than pass it to Derek—an outsider who didn't belong on this court with them.

Derek knew that it was happening, but he also knew it might not be obvious to any of the coaches.

"Yo, yo! Over here!" he called, only to be shunned yet again as the center took a difficult shot that was easily blocked.

By the time the coach signaled for Derek to come out and sent the starting point guard back in for him, the yellowshirts were trailing by eight points. They'd been tied when Derek entered the game.

He didn't get to play again until there were less than two minutes left. The yellowshirts were trailing by sixteen now, and his teammates were already looking defeated.

That made Derek mad. He was determined to at least make things close. He drove quickly upcourt and put up a midrange jumper. *Swish!* His first points of the game!

The other team walked the ball slowly up the court, killing the clock. Derek watched for an opportunity, and as soon as the ball handler wasn't looking, he snuck up behind him and knocked the ball away!

His teammate grabbed it and threw upcourt to the shooting guard, who laid the ball in.

Again, the blueshirts slow-walked the ball upcourt. Derek stuck ferociously to his man, harassing him so much that the kid committed a traveling violation. When the ref whistled it, he threw the ball down hard and gave Derek a withering look.

Derek looked away, not wanting to be diverted from his focus. Instead, he drove upcourt in a hurry, dished to the shooting guard, and watched him sink an open 3-pointer! Suddenly, with one minute left, the lead was down to 11!

The yellows narrowed the gap even further, but there wasn't enough time for them to really catch the blues. The game ended with Derek's team down by 6—but Derek felt better that at least he'd made a difference.

He hadn't shot very well, of course. Only 1 for 4—missing two that he should have made easily! But on the other hand, he'd done lots of other things right. He could only hope Coach Nelson had noticed.

"Nice game," said the yellow-shirted shooting guard. "You should try out next year."

"Thanks!" Derek said, finally flashing a smile. He glanced over at the coaches, but they were all busy making notes—except for Coach Nelson.

Where was he?

"Derek?"

Derek swung around to find the coach standing right behind him. "Hey, thanks for coming down tonight. You did well."

"Thanks, Coach." Derek waited for what the coach would say next.

"I'll . . . be making my decisions tomorrow regarding the under-twelve team," he said. "You can check the sheet in the lobby here after six p.m. Right now, though, I've got things to take care of with this team. So . . ."

"Right," Derek said, getting the picture. The rest of this practice would be private—and he and his parents weren't invited to stay.

Derek had been hoping the coach would tell him right there and then whether he'd made the team. Now he'd have to wait another whole other day!

He wasn't sure he could take the suspense.

Chapter Thirteen
UPS AND DOWNS

"Now, when he sings about the number on the dial, we should find a phone and pick it up—but the wire is just dangling, right? And the monster's getting closer and closer!"

"Right!" Vijay agreed. "So we'll need a phone with a ripped cord—and we can do some moves with it that'll be funny."

"And the monster can be holding the other part of the cord where he ripped it!" Derek threw in.

He and Vijay were going through their piece for the fifth time that afternoon, making little tweaks here and there. Each time, they would come up with new bits to add, to make the story clearer and funnier and scarier.

Vijay had learned all the moves Derek taught him, so now the two boys could move in unison or mirror each other.

Vijay's moves were harder for Derek to master—mainly because he'd gotten a late start and was only now beginning to learn them. Besides that, he was still going easy on his neck—just to make sure there was no problem when showtime came.

One more week. It felt like the show was right around the corner, but in reality he and Vijay would have plenty of time after school next week to practice. Derek felt pretty confident that they would do well—or at least not embarrass themselves. He'd been worried about that at first—in fact, it was only when they'd seen Gary do his thing that Derek stopped worrying about how it would go.

Gary's entrance was going to be the cherry on top! In fact, it would be sure to cause a total sensation!

So far, Gary had rehearsed with them only the one time, but his part was easy. There were no real break dance moves he had to do—just come onstage with a monster outfit and a ripped phone cord, and look and act scary. And then, of course, break into that crazy chicken dance!

"Shall we try the whole thing one more time?" Vijay asked, ready to hit the play button again.

"I don't think so, Vij," said Derek, looking at the clock on the living room wall. It was after five already. The team roster would be posted by six, the coach had promised.

Derek had been thinking about it all afternoon, even though he'd mostly put his anxiety aside so that he and Vijay could practice. But six o'clock was less than an hour away now—Derek knew he wouldn't be able to think about anything else till he knew his fate.

"I'm kind of played out. Let's pick it up again on Monday, when we have Gary here."

"Cool," said Vijay. "I am no longer worried about our success, now that we have rehearsed a bit. But you know what they say—"

"Practice makes perfect!" both boys said together.

"Hey!" Derek spotted Dave and Chase in the parking lot and trotted over to them while his dad locked the car.

"I guess you couldn't wait to see, any more than I could," Dave said as the two boys high-fived.

"No, man—the suspense is driving me crazy! Let's get in there!"

Chase shook hands with Mr. Jeter and clapped the two boys on the back.

"Good luck, men," he said. "And remember, you're already winners just by getting to the second round."

Chase and Mr. Jeter had been co-coaches of the boys' championship-winning Little League team last spring, and Derek really respected Chase. So they paid attention to what he said. Still, Derek knew that if his name wasn't up there with the rest, he'd feel totally crushed.

He was sure Dave had made the team, based on what he'd seen him do at tryouts. But Derek had had to prove himself on a much more difficult stage. And he'd missed all those easy shots, too!

They got to the lobby and stared at the list.

There was Dave's name, right at the top!

"Yeah! Congrats, man!" Derek told his friend, clapping him on the back.

At first, Derek didn't see his own name, and his heart began to sink. But then Dave pointed to it—right below Sam's. "Hey! You're in, Derek!"

"*YESSS!!* Whoo-hoo!!" Derek shouted, his arms raised in triumph.

He and Dave high-fived and hugged each other. Derek was out of his mind with relief and happiness. "This is amazing! We made it, Dave!"

"We're gonna rock it this season!"

Just then, Sam entered the building, accompanied by his mother.

"You made it, Sam!" Derek shouted, arms raised. "We all did!"

He showed Sam where his name was posted, under POINT GUARD—with Derek's right below it. Derek understood that this meant Sam would be the starter at the position and that he himself would be the backup. But, hey—so what if he started games on the bench? He'd been on the bench for his final tryout, too—and that hadn't stopped him from impacting the game, had it?

Derek felt a shot of pure happiness run through him. He knew there would be tough moments during the basketball season. But right now he was sitting on top of the world!

For the first time in two weeks he could relax and take pride in his accomplishments—at least for a little while.

The basketball season would not be starting for another week and a half. In the meantime, there would be practices, of course—but from now until next Friday night Derek's laser focus would be on the Fall Talent Show.

He owed that much to Vijay. But even more—he realized now that he owed it to *himself.*

That weekend the family watched Sharlee and her karate class put on a demonstration for the students' families. Sharlee was one of the youngest students, but she broke boards just like the rest of them—with an extra loud "Kee-yah!" to boot.

Derek and his parents stood and cheered, and Sharlee could not suppress a grin as she took her solemn karate bow.

The whole experience made Derek really look forward to Friday. He'd never competed in a talent show before. In fact, he'd never been onstage at all. The only time he'd ever performed was on a baseball field—and that was different.

But watching Sharlee do her thing had kind of given

him the "bug." She seemed so *relaxed* up there, so sure of herself.

Derek couldn't picture being *that* comfortable onstage. But during his and Vijay's rehearsals now, he was starting to get a sense of what it might be like to just *perform* and *enjoy* the experience, instead of getting all nervous about it.

"Mommy! Daddy! Ciara is doing indoor soccer this year! Can I do it too? And can we be on the same team? And can we be the red team? And—"

"Whoa! Whoa, there, girl!" said her dad, laughing. "Slow down!"

"What about your dance classes? And karate?" said Mrs. Jeter. "Are you going to be able to do everything and still get your schoolwork done?"

"Yeah, Sharlee," Derek agreed. "Don't you think you're maybe taking on too much at once?" "Like I did recently," he added silently.

"I can do *everything*!" Sharlee said, still floating on air from her demonstration of strength and power.

"Well, everything isn't *free*, you know," said Mr. Jeter. "But we'll talk about it. It sounds like something that might be a good fit."

"Plus it's on Saturdays!" Sharlee pointed out. "Right before Derek's basketball games."

"Sounds like you've already done your research," Mr. Jeter said, raising a surprised eyebrow.

"Uh-huh! Ciara is on the red team, so I want to be on it too."

"Well, we might not be able to arrange that part," Mrs. Jeter said with a laugh. "We're not all-powerful, you know."

"You *can* do it," Sharlee said with an air of certainty. "You and Daddy can do *anything*!"

"Wow, Derek! Looking good!" Vijay said as he watched Derek spin around on his back then flip back onto his feet. "Rock on!"

"It really is going to be good, isn't it?" Derek said. "I mean, it looks good to *me*. I don't know what else we could add at this point to make it better."

"Well, we do need to work Gary through his part a few more times."

"He promised to come tomorrow," Derek said.

"Well, he doesn't have as many pieces to work on as we do," Vijay said. "A couple times going through it should be enough."

"Okay, Vij. I guess we're done for today, then."

"See you tomorrow in school," said Vijay, high-fiving Derek. "Man, this really is going to be a *thriller*!"

"I quit."

Derek stood staring at Gary Parnell's impassive face. "Huh?"

"I said, 'I quit.' What part of 'I quit' don't you understand, Jeter?"

"What do you mean, you *quit*? You *can't* quit!"

"Oh, really? Who's going to stop me? *You?*"

"Gary, you *promised*! You can't back out now."

"Watch me."

"But *why*? You're doing great! You're going to be a hit, believe me!"

"A *hit*?" Gary snorted. "I think not. More like a crash and burn. Let me fill you in on my recent nights, Jeter. For your information, I have been enduring one awful nightmare after another. I wake up in a cold sweat, dreaming that the whole school is laughing at me!"

"Gary, come on . . . listen—"

"No, *you* listen, Mr. Busta Moves! One night I dreamed I was up there in nothing but my *underwear*—and there was a big rip in the back of my boxers! Another night—or maybe it was later the same night—I dreamed the *real* monster was chasing me down the school hallways. No matter how hard I ran, I kept going slower and slower, until he was right behind me, and I could feel him breathing down my neck!"

Other kids standing around them in the hallway turned to look, as Gary's voice broke the sound barrier in the echoing space.

Scowling back at them, Gary lowered his voice to a hush. "I'm *out*, that's all. Go find yourself another monster!"

"Great," said Derek, really steamed now. "This is just *great*. What are Vijay and I supposed to do without a monster? The show's only two days away!"

"I sympathize with your problem, Jeter," said Gary. "Boo-hoo. Lucky it's not *my* problem."

"But Gary, a promise is a promise! You can't go back on your word! Where's your self-respect?"

"Oh, no problem. I respect myself for being smart enough to know when to abandon a sinking ship."

"But—"

"Jeter, let me make it crystal clear for you. I can live with myself, backing out of a promise. What I can't live with is going up onstage Friday night and making a *complete spectacle* of myself—like you and Vijay are gonna do!"

Gary shrugged. "But hey—*enjoy*. And good luck—you're gonna need it! As for me, I'll be out there in the audience, laughing my head off like everybody else."

As Gary walked away, Derek heard him mutter, "Sheesh! Talent shows! What a waste of time and energy!"

Derek stared after him, a cold sweat breaking out on his forehead.

Now what were they going to do? How was he going to tell Vijay that their perfect monster had just vanished? And where were they going to get another kid to replace him, with just two days left before the show?

Chapter Fourteen

SCRAMBLE!

"Omigosh! What are we going to do? We're doomed!" Vijay held his hands to his ears as he paced back and forth, as if he didn't want to hear the bad news. Well, who could blame him?

Derek wasn't exactly dancing in the streets himself. Without Gary, their act seemed not only empty, but pointless! What was a horror scene without a monster? And Gary, though he couldn't dance in any meaningful sense of the word, was hilarious *trying* to—and that alone would have lifted the whole routine!

Now there was nothing but a blank where the heart of their dance had been. The whole story made no sense without the monster at the end.

"Do you think we should rework the whole thing?" Derek asked. "I mean, like, from scratch?"

"No way! No how!" Vijay said, clasping both hands together. "We have to find another monster—and fast!"

"But who?"

Vijay gave him a long look.

"No. Not Dave," Derek said. "I asked him first thing, remember? And he told me he would *never, ever* get up onstage and dance."

"But you and he are—well, second-best friends," said Vijay, who thought of *himself* as Derek's *very* best friend.

Derek felt equally close to both of them, but he couldn't help there being at least a little rivalry between Vijay and Dave over the amount of time they got to spend with Derek.

"I'm not asking him," Derek said. "You can if you want to."

"It won't do any good, me asking. And you know it." Vijay sat down on the couch, looking totally defeated.

Derek couldn't stand to see his friend that way. It broke his heart. "Okay, okay, I'll ask him," he finally said, causing Vijay to instantly brighten.

"It's our only hope!" Vijay said. "He will surely say yes. He cannot refuse you if you beg him."

"I'm not begging."

"You know what I mean," Vijay said, realizing he'd used the wrong word.

"I'll ask him. If he says no, that's it."

"Yes . . . that really will be it. I think we will have to withdraw from the competition in that case."

Wow. Derek hadn't thought of it quite like that till now. After they'd put in so much work—and had so many great ideas . . . to just drop out at the last minute would be a crushing blow!

Derek would survive. After all, he'd still be on the AAU under-12 basketball team. With Dave.

But where would Vijay be? This talent show was going to be his new claim to fame at Saint Augustine's.

Derek couldn't let his buddy down—he *had* to find a monster!

He was pretty sure Dave would say no, though.

And who was he going to ask *then*?

"I'm really sorry, Derek. I get it about Vijay. I wish I could help you both. But there's just no way. I *can't*. You don't understand the feeling I get in the pit of my stomach whenever I even *think* about it!"

"I *do* understand," Derek said. "I mean, I'm that way myself when it comes to getting up in front of the class and giving a speech. Don't you remember in fourth grade when—"

"That was before I moved here, remember?"

"Oh. Right. Of course. Well, it happened, believe me. And it wasn't pretty. I can get up there if I'm dancing, but don't ask me to talk."

Dave gave him a smile, and Derek went on. "Look, I

know how you feel, believe me. But you can't let your fear stop you, Dave! If you want to ever get past it and succeed, you can't be afraid to fail."

"You sound like your mom or dad," Dave said.

Derek felt himself blushing. He'd heard that advice from one or both of them, for sure.

But he *wasn't* just repeating it from memory. He *believed* it. He'd wanted to back out of this talent show early on himself, hadn't he? But he'd stuck with it, and he was glad he did!

At least, he *had* been glad—until *now*.

"Sorry, Derek. I really am sorry. I owe you one—just . . . not *this* one."

Derek sighed deeply as he watched Dave walk away down the hallway.

"Hey, Derek. What's up?"

Derek swung around and found himself face-to-face with Sam Rockman.

"Oh—hi, Sam!"

"You okay, man?"

"Yeah! Fine! Why do you ask?"

"I don't know. . . . I mean, we're on the team together, dude! Is that great, or what?"

"Yeah!" Derek high-fived Sam, who was obviously in a great mood.

"So your mom decided to let you play, huh? That's fantastic!"

"Yeah! And it's only because of you, dude. If not for you,

I'd have been all scheduled up with tutoring, extra home-work—ugh! I can't thank you enough."

And that gave Derek a great idea.

"Well, actually, if you *wanted* to thank me . . . I've got a way."

"Yeah? Okay, name it!"

"*Really?* Are you *sure*?"

"As long as it doesn't interfere with me playing on the team."

"No, no, nothing like that. In fact, you'll be done with this by Friday night."

"Cool!" said Sam. "Count me in. What do I have to do?"

"Just come on by my house after school," said Derek, a sly grin spreading over his face, "and I'll show you."

Chapter Fifteen

ON WITH THE SHOW!

Vijay looked shocked when Sam rang the bell at Derek's house. "What are you doing here, Sam?" he asked.

Sam shrugged. "Derek said to be here, so I'm here."

"Welcome!" Vijay said, ushering Sam inside. "You are *most, most* welcome!"

Sam took a seat on the couch, and Derek proceeded to explain why he was there.

"Oh. Wow," said Sam, his good mood fading in a hurry. "Aw, guys, I don't know. It's kind of . . . last-minute, isn't it? I would need a lot of practice to do something like that."

"No, you wouldn't," Derek assured him. "Sam, I've seen your moves—on the basketball court. All you have to do is put on some monster makeup and a cape and pretend you're driving the lane—in slow motion!"

"Huh?"

"Hey, if it doesn't work, we'll try something else," said Derek. "But at least you'll be doing something you're used to."

They tried it out—and it kind of worked okay. But then Sam said, "You know, it might be better if I had an actual basketball."

"I don't think so," Vijay said. "The audience wouldn't get it. Just *pretend* you do."

"It'll look pretty weird," said Sam.

"Oh, don't worry," Vijay assured him. "In this case, weird is good! You're a monster, remember? Monsters are supposed to be weird."

"Oh. Well, okay, then. Let's try it one more time."

He wasn't Gary—but Sam seemed to get the general idea. After the first couple of times, he even got into it a little bit.

After half an hour, it was time for Sam to leave. But as he was going, he had one more thing to say. "Just so you guys know—I mean, so you're not surprised when I mess up—I've never been in front of an audience before, other than in a basketball game."

After he left, Derek and Vijay looked at each other. "Well, you know what they say," Derek offered. "Ninety percent of life is just showing up. He's got Gary beat there!"

• • •

The school parking lot was mobbed. Derek stared out through the drops of rain that coated the car windows. It was going to be a full house tonight.

Well, he wasn't surprised. There was a lot of talent at Saint Augustine's school, and all that talent had parents, grandparents, cousins, uncles, aunts, and lots and lots of friends.

"I'm so excited!" Sharlee piped up, clapping her hands. "My brother is going to be the star of the whole show!"

"Don't jinx me," Derek told her, although he grinned when he said it.

He was nervous, of course. More so every minute as the time crept closer. But he loved his sister's confidence in him. It was like listening to Vijay. Both of them always thought things were going to turn out great.

Vijay had had a few dark moments over this show, for sure. But today in school, he'd once again been like his usual self—upbeat and confident about their chances. Gary's desertion had sent Vijay into a tailspin. Sam's arrival had lifted him right back up again.

As for Derek, he was trying to keep on more of an even keel. Every night this week he'd dreamt of things going wrong—just like Gary had. He only hoped those dreams didn't predict the future.

At any rate, there was no turning back now. Derek kept repeating all the things his parents had told him: "If you give it your best, you haven't failed." "Mistakes are there to learn from so you can improve." "The only failure is not even trying."

He knew it was all true. *So why didn't it help him now?*

He was as nervous as he could ever remember being. Even in a championship baseball game, he seemed to be able to hold it together and focus so that he could come through in the clutch.

But this was different. This was not baseball. It wasn't even basketball! It wasn't something he'd been practicing and working at his entire life—it was totally, terrifyingly new. Sure, he'd danced before, but only at home, or once or twice at people's weddings or birthday parties.

"Here we are!" Mrs. Jeter said. "You take the kids inside, Jeter," she told her husband. "I'll park the car."

The three of them got out and ran through the rain to the front door of the school, while Mrs. Jeter continued on, looking for a parking spot.

"Derek, you've got to get backstage," said his dad. "Good luck, son. You're going to be just fine." He held Derek by both shoulders and looked him right in the eye. "Just focus on doing the routine. The rest will follow naturally."

"First place or bust!" Sharlee chirped, hugging Derek.

"Sharlee, come on now," Derek said. "Just clap loud, okay?"

"Uh-huh!"

"Come on, Sharlee," said Mr. Jeter. "Let's go find some good seats for us and Mom."

Vijay was backstage, hopping up and down to use up his excess energy. "Derek!" he called, waving. "Over here!"

The stage at Saint Augustine's was large, but the back-stage area was tight and crowded with props. "Where are we supposed to hang out till our entrance?" Derek asked.

"Downstairs in the cafeteria," said Vijay. "But I wanted to make sure our set was ready."

"Our *set*? *What* set?"

"See this door?" Vijay showed Derek a freestanding doorframe. "When we open this door, Sam will be stand-ing there, in full costume!"

"Great!" Derek said. "Where'd you manage to get this?"

"Sally Spitzer is the stage manager for the drama club—she hooked me up with it."

Sally lived in Mount Royal Townhouses, right next door to Vijay. She made her own go-karts and could fix any-thing broken.

"Nice!" Derek said.

"She's going to run our spotlight, too!" Vijay said. "I told her to keep it on Sam once he comes out."

"Speaking of Sam . . . where is he?" Derek asked.

Vijay frowned. "I haven't seen him . . . but I'm sure he'll be here. . . . You don't think he would—"

"Drop out on us? Not a chance," Derek said. "I did him a

solid last month, helping him out on those tests. He won't let us down, don't worry."

Derek tried the doorknob. "Cool. Who's going to open it—me or you?"

"I think you should do it," Vijay said. "I'm supposed to be the timid one, remember?" It was the way they'd laid out the story—Derek convincing Vijay to make a bad choice, daring him to enter the haunted house.

"Well, hello there, suckers!"

"Gary!" Derek said. "What are *you* doing back here?"

"Just wanted to wish you two the best of luck—you're totally going to need it! *Ha!*"

"I'm surprised you didn't just stay home," Derek said. "Since you think talent shows are such a waste of time."

"He thinks *everything* is a waste of time," Vijay said with a touch of bitterness.

"Not *everything*," Gary said. "Just everything *you* two clowns are into."

"I think he just dropped out because he was too chicken," Derek told Vijay.

"*Chicken?* Well, I call it *smart*," said Gary, unconvinced. "And the only reason I bothered to brave the rainstorm to come here is that I wanted to see for myself just how big a disaster I got myself out of!"

"You got yourself out of it by *breaking your word*," Derek reminded him. "You're going to have to live with that, one way or the other."

"No problem," said Gary. "I can live with being a cop-out—it beats making a fool out of myself in front of everyone I know." He sniggered. "Well, I'd better go find myself a front row seat."

He laughed—the same laugh he'd used as the monster—and left the two of them there, alone in the semidarkness.

"I can't stand that guy," Vijay said.

"Ah, he's not all bad."

"No?"

"Nah. Remember how he helped our team win the Little League championship?"

"He *had* to do that! His mother made him play!"

"Yeah, but he could have dropped that fly ball on purpose. It was the biggest catch of the whole season. That's got to count for something."

"Says you. I say he's my least favorite person in our whole class."

Derek sighed. "Never mind him. Let's make him eat his words, huh?"

"Right!" Vijay said, giving Derek a smile. "And when we win the first prize trophy, we will bring it to class and put it right on his desk, so he can see it up close!"

If Derek had been nervous before, when he got to the cafeteria and saw all the kids who were going to be their competition, he really started to sweat.

Harry Chen was there with his guitar—Derek had

heard him play once in the music room, and he was incredible. Daisy Hargrove had been taking voice lessons since she was five years old—she'd already played two leads in musicals at the local community theater. Eva Katz was in her toe shoes, ready to show everybody her ballet moves. All these kids seemed calm and ready, primed to do their best.

Could Derek and Vijay stand up to the competition?

And *where was Sam*?

When Mrs. Seymour came downstairs and called for the first three acts to follow her upstairs, it was seven fifteen. The show was supposed to have started at seven, but these kinds of shows always started late.

A good thing too—because where was Sam? "He can't have forgotten about it," Derek said aloud.

Vijay knew exactly whom Derek was talking about. "We don't know Sam that well. Maybe he just decided not to come. Or chickened out, like Gary."

"I still say he'll be here."

"And if he's not? What do we do then? We're listed as going on fifteenth. I'm thinking that's in about forty-five minutes, right? If he's not here in fifteen, I suggest we tell Mrs. Seymour. She'll know what to do."

"Maybe she'll let us go last or something," Derek said hopefully.

"Or *something* . . . ," Vijay echoed, his voice trailing off to a whisper.

"Mi, mi, mi, miiii . . . mi, mi, mi!" sang Daisy Hargrove, warming up her voice.

Wow, thought Derek. *She sure can hit a high note. . . .*

Eva Katz did a few pirouettes, and Harry Chen tuned up his guitar, playing some amazing riffs just to warm up his fingers.

"Show-offs, all of them," Vijay muttered. But neither he nor Derek got up to practice any of their dance moves.

No one knew what kind of act they were about to perform. Derek and Vijay had kept it a complete secret. The only thing anyone knew about it was that the song "Thriller" was involved—and even that was only because it had to be listed in the program.

Mrs. Seymour came down and got the next three performers.

"Where are the first three?" Vijay wondered. "What happened to them?"

"I think you can go out and sit in the back of the audience after you're done," Derek said. "Hey, we'd better get in costume, huh?"

"For sure!" said Vijay, glad to have something to do except worry.

They grabbed their backpacks and headed for the boys' room. There, Derek changed into his outfit—warm-up gear with cool stripes down the shirtsleeves and pant legs, all in black, silver, and gold.

Vijay stepped out of the stall where he had gone to change.

"Wow!" Derek gasped. "Awesome, Vij!"

"You think so? Me too!" Vijay looked like a Bollywood

superstar. He wore a red spangled jacket, bright blue pants, and sneakers that were painted gold. On top of it, he sported *huge* sunglasses, with a silver star over each eye!

"Okay!" Derek said. "Let's go get 'em!" They went back into the cafeteria, drawing stares from the other performers who were still waiting their turn.

Sure, they both looked good. But time was passing by, and still no Sam. It was already 7:35, and the second hand kept on circling round and round, round and round.

Where was he?

Now Derek was starting to get spooked out for real. He'd been sure Sam wouldn't back out of his commitment. But Vijay was right—neither of them knew Sam that well. Anything was possible. . . .

Numbers seven through nine were called, then ten through twelve.

"Mrs. Seymour?" Derek finally asked. "Um, we're missing one of our performers."

"Well, now is a fine time to tell me," she said huffily. "You and Vijay are the only ones listed on the program. . . ."

"Yes, but we have a surprise guest star," Vijay said. "And he's not here!"

"Can't you go on without him?"

"No!" Vijay said. "It's not possible!"

"Well, you still have a little time," she said. "Who is this mystery guest, may I ask?"

"Sam Rockman," Derek said.

"Oh! Why didn't you say so?" she asked. "Sam's been sitting backstage for the past hour—he's in costume and makeup and didn't want anyone to see what he looked like before the show!"

Derek and Vijay looked at each other, a flood of relief coursing through them. "Makeup?" Vijay repeated. "He didn't say anything about makeup. . . ."

"Well, be prepared," she told them. "I had quite a shock myself when I saw him!"

It was as if new life had been injected into both the boys. Derek suddenly couldn't sit still. He started doing stretches, bouncing up and down, spinning around once or twice, doing a little moonwalking.

Vijay, too, was all motion. It was practically deserted down here now, with twelve of the contestants already gone.

Mrs. Seymour appeared again. "Thirteen, fourteen, and fifteen," she announced. "Come with me, please."

Harry Chen got up and slung his guitar over his shoulder. Daisy Hargrove cleared her throat. And Derek and Vijay followed them up the stairs.

"I can't wait to see what Sam looks like!" Vijay said.

"I sure hope whatever he did looks good," Derek agreed.

They need not have worried. Sam was not only in full costume, with a black cape and top hat—he was also in complete clown white makeup, except for black circles around his eyes and black lips that made his teeth stand out like fangs! He'd even pasted long, sharp, fake nails onto his fingertips!

"Hi, guys!" he said. "Ready to go. You?"

"Boy, are we glad to see you!" Derek said.

"You look horrible!" Vijay said. "It's fantastic!"

"Thanks!" Sam said. "Grrrr!" He stuck his fingernails out at them, and both boys giggled softly.

"SSSHhh!" said Harry Chen, who was awaiting his turn to go on.

Derek and Vijay put fingers to their mouths, but they couldn't hide their smiles.

Harry blew the audience away, playing some Jimi Hendrix song that went so fast it was totally dazzling. The crowd shouted and gave him a standing ovation, and Harry came offstage wearing a smile that practically screamed *I win!*

Not to be outdone, Daisy Hargrove went out there and sang an aria. Her high note at the end made a glass of water that was standing on a table backstage rattle and buzz—luckily, it didn't break.

It was the boys' turn next. The door was rolled into place at one end of the stage. Vijay placed Sam behind it and gave a nod to the stage manager, who returned it with a thumbs-up.

The music started. Derek sashayed his way onstage—Mister Cool—and did a double-spin move just to kick things off. The crowd whooped and hollered—at least his family and friends did. Derek could see Sharlee, and he knew his parents would be right next to her.

He looked down at the front row, and there were Vijay's parents—right next to Gary, who had a big smirk on his face. Derek didn't care—he was ready to show Gary what dancing was all about.

He did a floor spin, causing another round of whoops and applause. Then Vijay came on—and the crowd really began to get into it.

Derek was known around the school as an athlete and one of the "smart kids." But it would have surprised no one to find out he could break-dance.

Vijay, on the other hand, was known as a brainiac and a class clown who loved to laugh and tell jokes. To see him break-dancing up onstage came as a complete surprise. And to see him do it this well? Awesome!

Now the story the two boys had come up with began to play out. Derek mimed his own bravery, daring Vijay to approach the haunted house with him. Vijay pretended not to be scared, mimicking every dance move Derek tried, just to show he was no slacker.

But as they approached the door, and the song lyrics warned of impending doom, Vijay pretended to back off, doing a cool glide step backward while Derek moonwalked forward alone.

At last, with the crowd now really into it, Derek looked at the poster of the haunted house, pulled on the doorknob, and yanked it open.

Sally flicked on the spotlight—and there was Sam, monster deluxe, baring his fingernails and teeth in the open doorway as Derek and Vijay did backflips and the worm.

The crowd practically screamed at their first sight of Sam—then started clapping rhythmically along with the music as Sam danced his monster dance, slowly approaching the two terrified intruders.

It turned out that Sam had some really amazing moves of his own too—moves he hadn't shown in rehearsal with Derek and Vijay!

At the end of the number the three boys froze in mid-move. The audience rose as one, giving them a loud, long, standing ovation!

Derek could barely hear anything but the thumping of his own heart and the rushing breath in his ears. He looked over at Vijay, who was beaming, and at Sam, who was still making monster gestures to the crowd.

Geez, Derek thought. *What a ham he turned out to be—who would have thought it?*

They bowed and bowed, then ran offstage and hugged one another.

"SSSHHHH!" This time it was Eva Katz, about to do her ballet piece.

Derek motioned for them to leave the backstage area. Vijay and Sam followed him through the hall to the back of the auditorium, where they entered and stood behind the last row of seats with all the other kids who'd finished performing.

"Man, that was so awesome!" Vijay whispered, high-fiving Derek. "And Sam, you were amazing!"

"Aw, come on," Sam said. "That was nothing."

"Hey," Derek said. "That was not nothing. It meant a lot, Sam."

"Well, then, now we're even," said Sam. "See you on the court at practice."

He clapped Derek on the back and shook hands with Vijay. "Good luck, you guys. I've got to fly. I told my mom to pick me up at eight thirty."

"What? You mean, your parents didn't come to the show?"

"Nah," said Sam. "I actually told them I was here to watch some friends perform. She doesn't know I was in it."

"Why didn't you tell her?" Derek asked, confounded.

Sam shrugged. "No big deal," he said. "I'm not really into performing."

"You could have fooled me," Vijay said. "In fact, you *did* fool me—you fooled *everybody*!"

"SHHHH!" Now it was Sally Spitzer, wielding her spotlight, who ordered them to hush up.

Sam took off with a wave, and the two boys watched the rest of the talent show.

When it was over, Mrs. Seymour came out onstage to announce the winners.

"You were soooo great!" Eva Katz whispered to Daisy

Hargrove as they stood next to Derek and Vijay. "I'm sure you're going to win!"

"No, I'm sure *you* are," Daisy whispered back. "I mean, you were *incredible*!"

"You too!"

"You too!"

The two girls hugged and held hands, staring up at Mrs. Seymour, who was squinting in the light of Sally's spotlight. "Our third place winner is . . . Eva Katz!"

Everyone applauded, and many in the crowd stood up and whooped as Eva hugged Daisy yet again, this time with a tear in her eye, and proceeded to walk down the aisle, waving at the crowd on her way to pick up her trophy.

"Wasn't she amazing?" Mrs. Seymour asked the crowd, which responded with more cheers.

"She *won* the last two years in a row," Daisy muttered. "It's *about time* someone else had a turn."

"Second place goes to . . . Harry Chen!" Mrs. Seymour announced. "Wasn't he wonderful? Let's hear it for him, everyone!"

The crowd cheered Harry loudly. Daisy, however, seemed anxious. She wore a confused look on her face, in spite of her plastered-on smile. Derek understood how she felt. With Eva out of the way, Daisy must have assumed she was either second or first. Now second was gone. Which surely meant she would nail the ultimate prize.

Right?

Vijay gripped Derek's arm. "Here it comes!" he murmured, unable to contain his excitement.

Derek wished his friend would tone it down a little. After all, there were twenty other contestants who might come out on top. He and Vijay had gotten to hear only a few. And Daisy hadn't even been mentioned yet.

"Our first place this year ended up in a tie!" Mrs. Seymour announced delightedly. "Yes! We have *two* winners—both very different, and both equally worthy! First, Daisy Hargrove!"

Daisy screamed, both hands to her cheeks, and practically ran down the aisle to grab her trophy. Everyone applauded, but the show wasn't quite over—not yet.

"And our *other* first-place winner—or should I say 'winners'—are Derek Jeter, Vijay Patel—and their surprise guest, Sam Rockwell, for 'Thriller'! Wasn't it thrilling?"

"*Yes!!! I knew it! I knew it!* Didn't I tell you, Derek?"

"You called it, Vij!" Derek couldn't believe they'd won. His cheeks felt numb—in fact, his whole body felt like it was floating!

The rest was more or less a blur. They were serenaded by cheers all the way down the aisle and up onto the stage. Mrs. Seymour handed the two of them a trophy that looked just like an Oscar. "And where is Sam?" she asked Derek as he stood next to her in front of the mic.

"He, um, he had to go," Derek said. Then he turned to the audience. "Sam couldn't be here to accept the trophy, but, believe me, we're going to share it with him at school, first thing Monday morning!"

Chapter Sixteen

JUST REWARDS

When the tie for first place had been announced, Derek wasn't the only one who was shocked. But once the initial buzz of shock passed, everyone had clapped and cheered for the winners.

Everyone, that is, except for one person. There, slouched in his seat in the front row, sat Gary—who looked as if he had just swallowed a huge helping of turtle guts.

He didn't get up to go—probably because he would have stood out like a sore thumb. He'd chosen to sit in the first row, just so he could enjoy himself to the max watching Derek and Vijay go down in flames.

And now the joke was on him.

But Derek wasn't mad. Not anymore. In fact, he felt

kind of sorry for Gary as he watched him squirm in his seat.

"Not bad for a pair of newbies and a last-minute walk-on, huh?" Vijay said, clapping Derek on the arm. "Hi, Momma! Hi, Poppy!" he yelled, waving to his parents—who *still* looked shell-shocked, but also happy and proud.

Derek guessed that Vijay had kept things a total surprise for them until now—after all, the rehearsals had all been at Derek's place.

Vijay went over to greet them, and Derek stepped off the stage, only to find himself facing Gary.

"Well, Jeter," he said, offering his hand. "Congratulations."

"Thanks, Gary," Derek said, stunned.

"I guess there's just no accounting for taste."

Derek laughed as he shook his rival's hand. "I guess not. Sorry you decided to quit. You could have been the star of the show."

"Oh, I don't care," said Gary—who obviously did. "I've learned from this experience, and that's what counts."

"Oh yeah? Good! What did you learn?"

"I learned that I was right—being onstage is totally lame. Almost as lame as playing sports."

"Oooh-kay . . . ," said Derek, backing away slowly. "Well, I'll see you in school on Monday, Gar. I've . . . got to go say hi to my folks."

Poor Gary, he thought as he made his way across the aisle. *This has to be a hard night for him.*

Derek's parents were standing next to Vijay's, hugging each other and shaking hands.

When he got off the stage and reached them, his dad announced, "We're all going over to Jahn's for ice cream sundaes to celebrate. Great job, boys. We're all proud of you!"

Dave was there, too, along with his parents—and Chase! Derek hadn't realized they would all be there to see the show. "Just because I was too chicken to get up there didn't mean I wasn't going to come root for my best bud," Dave told him.

"Thanks," Derek said. "I wish you would have been in it, though—it would have been so cool."

"Yeah? I don't think so. Anyway, Sam was mind-blowing! Who would have thought he had it in him?"

"I know! Right?" Derek had to laugh along with Dave at the thought. "He wasn't my first choice, believe me—or even my second."

He didn't tell Dave who the second choice had been. He figured Gary was feeling bad enough already. Why make it worse by telling more people?

"Nice trophy!" Dave told Vijay, who had come up beside them. "Wow—you guys are so multitalented! Who knew?"

"That's just it," Derek said. "You never know until you try. Right, Vij?"

"You can say that again!" Vijay agreed, giving the trophy a kiss.

"So, who's going to get to keep it?" Dave asked. "Too bad they only gave you one."

Derek and Vijay looked at each other. "You keep it, Derek," Vijay said.

"No, Vij. This whole thing was your idea."

"No, Derek, we both came up with lots of good ideas!"

Then both boys came up with the same solution. "Sam!"

"You're going to give it to Sam?" Dave said, surprised. "But he only had that short bit at the end. Sure, it was amazing, but—"

"He saved our act," Vijay said. "Otherwise, we wouldn't have won."

"Come on, you guys," Derek said, "let's all go get some dessert—we've got a lot to celebrate!"

Derek lay in bed with the lights out, feeling like he had a bowling ball in his stomach. Of course, it was only four scoops of ice cream, along with a big helping of satisfaction. He might not be able to eat again for a week—but tonight's celebration had been worth it!

He'd never imagined, way back during the summer, when he'd fantasized with his friends about talent shows and basketball teams, that he would be here in early October with a golden trophy *and* a spot on the basketball team!

None of it had been easy, either. Almost everything that could have gone wrong *had* gone wrong.

He might easily have failed to make the team—in fact, he *almost had.*

He and Vijay might have had to cancel their routine when they couldn't find a monster—but they'd found Sam in the end.

They might have forgotten or blown a dance move in the middle of the performance—*but they hadn't.*

And *if* they had? If he had *failed* at one or more of his efforts?

But that was just it, Derek realized now. Even if he hadn't made the team, or won the talent show, or beaten Gary out on those tests—he *still* wouldn't have failed. Not *really*. Look at all he'd learned along the way—including how to budget his time better!

No, the only failure would have been if he was *too scared to even try*—if he'd turned down the chance to be in the talent show, just because he might fail. Or if he hadn't bothered to show up for tryouts, lest someone beat him out for the spot on the team.

"You can't succeed if you don't try," he said to himself, thinking of Gary Parnell. "Oh well—it takes all kinds to make a world."

He closed his eyes and let himself drift off toward sleep.

Tomorrow was the start of the new basketball season! Dreams of on-court heroics with Dave and Sam filled his head. . . .

"He shoots . . . he SCORES!!!"

JETER PUBLISHING

Jeter Publishing's sixth middle-grade book is inspired by the childhood of Derek Jeter, who grew up playing baseball. The middle-grade series is based on the principles of Jeter's Turn 2 Foundation.

Jeter Publishing encompasses adult nonfiction, children's picture books, middle-grade fiction, ready-to-read children's books, and children's nonfiction.

JETER'S LEADERS

is a leadership development program created to empower, recognize, and enhance the skills of high school students who:

- **PROMOTE HEALTHY LIFESTYLES AND ARE FREE OF ALCOHOL AND SUBSTANCE ABUSE**

- **ACHIEVE ACADEMICALLY**

- **ARE COMMITTED TO IMPROVING THEIR COMMUNITY THROUGH SOCIAL CHANGE ACTIVITIES**

- **SERVE AS ROLE MODELS TO YOUNGER STUDENTS AND DELIVER POSITIVE MESSAGES TO THEIR PEERS**

About the Authors

DEREK JETER played Major League Baseball for the New York Yankees for twenty seasons and is a five-time World Series champion. He is a true legend in professional sports and a role model for young people on and off the field and through his work in the community with his Turn 2 Foundation. For more information, visit Turn2Foundation.org.

Derek was born in New Jersey and moved to Kalamazoo, Michigan, when he was four. There he often attended Detroit Tigers games with his family, but the New York Yankees were always his favorite team, and he never stopped dreaming of playing for them.

PAUL MANTELL is the author of more than one hundred books for young readers.